ESCAPE FROM THE WILDFIRE

DOROTHY BENTLEY

James Lorimer & Company Ltd., Publishers
Toronto

*This story is dedicated to the survivors of the
Lytton wildfire, 2021.*

James Lorimer & Company Ltd., Publishers acknowledges funding support from
the Ontario Arts Council (OAC), an agency of the Government of Ontario. We
acknowledge the support of the Canada Council for the Arts, which last year
invested $153 million to bring the arts to Canadians throughout the country. This
project has been made possible in part by the Government of Canada and with
the support of Ontario Creates.

Cover design: Tyler Cleroux
Cover image: Shutterstock

Library and Archives Canada Cataloguing in Publication

Title: Escape from the wildfire / Dorothy Bentley.
Names: Bentley, Dorothy, author.
Identifiers: Canadiana (print) 20220273073 | Canadiana (ebook) 2022027309X
    | ISBN 9781459417021 (softcover) | ISBN 9781459417038 (hardcover)
    | ISBN 9781459417045 (EPUB)
Classification: LCC PS8603.E5789 E83 2022 | DDC jC813/.6—dc23

Published by:
James Lorimer & Company
Ltd., Publishers
117 Peter Street, Suite 304
Toronto, ON, Canada
M5V 0M3
www.lorimer.ca

Distributed in Canada by:
Formac Lorimer Books
5502 Atlantic Street
Halifax, NS, Canada
B3H 1G4
www.formaclorimerbooks.ca

Distributed in the US by:
Lerner Publisher Services
241 1st Ave. N.
Minneapolis, MN, USA
55401
www.lernerbooks.com

Printed and bound in Canada.
Manufactured by Friesens in Altona, MB in August 2022.
Job #291901

CONTENTS

THE LYTTON WILDFIRE, 2021
PROLOGUE
June 30, 2021

I run up the stairs. Scott follows. My heart pounds like a locomotive. The house is full of smoke. Angry flames roil, consuming the house. Thoughts come like fragments of movies and games. *We're under attack.* I half expect military guys to jump out from the flames with submachine guns, but this is no game.

"JACK! THE HOUSE IS ON FIRE! GET OUT!" Glenda yells.

"What's happening?" Scott stumbles into me as he emerges from the basement.

"Outside, NOW!" Glenda yells.

Did I leave the coffee maker on when I made iced coffees? Did I forget to turn something off? This is the first time I've been allowed to stay at home while Mom and Dad and Quinn are all away. This can't be happening. This is the first day of summer holidays. This is all my fault. I must have done something wrong.

I cough and cough, my lungs suck air. My eyes and throat burn. I can hardly see the door through the smoke. I run my hands along the hallway wall, feeling my way to the door. The door is open, and I rush toward it. I turn back to look for my friend.

"Scott! Where are you?" I can't see him.

Suddenly, Scott rushes past me. Both of us race down the wooden stoop to the front yard. The brittle lawn stabs my bare feet and I stare at the house. Flames jump along the roof. The trees next to us are like tiki torches.

"My shoes! My shoes! I need my runners!" I rush back inside the house and Scott follows. Right inside the door, I look down at the linoleum. I see my shoes, so I pick them up and stop, staring at the red-hot orange flames. Scott grabs his shoes, too, and we are mesmerized. Frozen in a bizarre scene. Fear grips me, and I can't move.

MONDAY JULY 19

twenty days after the wildfire

When I close my eyes to sleep, I see flames and think the fire is coming.

My counselor, Stephanie, said, "Jack, write your story of loss, and I'll help you with the punctuation. You'll never do well in school if you don't learn where to put commas."

"Whatever," I said. I do care, but I didn't want to admit it to her.

Mr. Marconi, my old English teacher, didn't teach about commas. I mean, I could have asked him to help me, and he would have, except I don't know where he went when everyone evacuated. I said goodbye to him on June 29, the last day of school, and on June 30, Lytton was annihilated.

Stephanie said to focus on things related to the fire. When I think about it, everything about Lytton is related to the fire, and the fire changed everything.

SATURDAY MARCH 6

three months, three weeks and two days before the wildfire

"Take out the trash, Jack," my dad said. It was a Saturday, and it was close to noon. I'd slept in because I was up until 1:00 a.m. gaming with Rory and Scott.

My dad stretched in front of the kitchen window before returning his attention to the stove. "We sure needed that rain."

"Why do you have to ruin your future?" my mom exploded at Quinn. Mom stood next to the propane stove where Dad continued cooking breakfast. It felt like I'd walked into a bees' nest, but the smell of bacon had awoken me. The white stained coffee maker gurgled at its spot on the counter, while Mom waited with her empty cup. Dad refused to give up the old appliance any time Mom pressured him.

"Why don't you bug Jack about *his* future?" Quinn

calmly retrieved her toast and spread it with almond butter. She bumped me with her hip and winked at me with a slight smile, then poured herself a cup of coffee. Quinn was laid back about everything. She liked to take things as they came in life.

"Hey, leave me out of this," I told her, rubbing my eyes. Then to my parents I said, "By the way, I need a camera for photography class." I poured cereal into a bowl, preparing my pre-breakfast snack. Through the kitchen window, the mountains across the Fraser River no longer had any snow. It had melted weeks ago. It was already shaping up to be a warm spring in the valley. I was excited because as soon as the mud dried up from the one rainy day, the trails would be good for biking again.

I sat next to Quinn at the table, waiting for Dad to finish making bacon and eggs.

"You can have my old cell phone," Quinn offered. "It takes decent photos. It's on my bedside table." She flipped through the tree-planting guide she'd received in the mail. It was called *Step by Step, a Tree Planter's Guide*. She'd also ordered a tree planter's fitness guide called *Fit to Plant* to get into shape.

"Cool, thanks," I said and went to get the phone from her basement bedroom.

"Don't forget the power cord, Jack," she called down the stairs.

I found the phone right away, then tried several charger cords, which I pulled from under her bedside table. Once I found the right cord, I took both phone and charger back to the kitchen. The phone powered on fine, and I found the photo app and opened it. I snapped a picture of Quinn, which she wasn't expecting. She had on a faded blue ten-tree t-shirt, and her cropped blonde hair was messy and a little uneven. She cut her own hair because she thought hairdressers charged too much. She took after Dad in the looks department, and I took after Mom.

Mom filled her coffee cup and joined us at the table. "Tree planting is for people who can't get other jobs." She pressured Quinn non-stop to go to university and reach for a profession. Professions are big in her family. "Your grandfather was a doctor, and your aunt is a lawyer in Victoria," she liked to remind us.

"I planted trees for two summers," Dad said. "All sorts of people do it." He loaded a platter with crisp bacon, half a dozen sunny-side-up eggs and orange wedges. He set it in the middle of the table.

"You were in college, and you knew it was temporary. She'll get stuck in it."

"It doesn't matter. I don't want a typical job," Quinn said calmly, reading her guide while munching her toast. "I want to plant trees during the summer and work on my design business the rest of the year." Quinn had signed up for online high school since the beginning of the pandemic, and she'd finished early. She liked setting her own schedule, since she designed and sewed clothes from old garments and made homemade soaps and shampoos. She'd begun selling them in a shop on Main Street. I loved the soaps and shampoos. They were all I used. My favourite was the peppermint shampoo.

"What's wrong with typical?" Mom huffed.

"Now, calm down, Cindy," Dad said. He offered her a plate loaded with food and she took it.

"Don't tell me to calm down! She's wasting her life, Rob." Mom's voice grew louder.

"Have you looked at schools, Quinn?" Dad said in between bites of bacon.

I loaded my plate with bacon and eggs, slipped my new cell phone camera into my pocket and headed for the basement rec room. I hated listening to my parents hound Quinn. I'd been in and out of school since the start of the pandemic. I would have done online school, too, except I liked seeing my friends when school was in person. On my way downstairs, I grabbed my hoodie off the living room sofa. It was chilly in the basement.

"Don't forget to practice guitar," Mom called.

I didn't feel like telling my mom yet that I'd quit going to guitar lessons last week. I wasn't interested anymore. It was going to be nice outside soon, nice enough to go mountain biking every day. She'd know soon enough and then she'd pressure me to start back up. I already knew lots of songs, and I knew I didn't want to play music professionally, so why bother?

Once my game system booted up, I put on my headphones and focused on gaming.

THURSDAY APRIL 1

two months, four weeks before the wildfire

I'd always hated English class until this year because Mr. Marconi was my teacher at Kumsheen ShchEma-meet School. My class moved into the new school in January. It was kindergarten to grade twelve, and lots of kids in town and from the surrounding areas went there. It was okay. I liked the new padded seats in the hallway where we hung out, and I liked the new skylights.

My mom is a teacher at my school. She was all excited about the new library because they'd ordered a bunch of graphic novels. "You'll like them," she said. She drank coffee and loaded the dishwasher.

"We'll see," I told her. "No promises."

"You quit guitar lessons, Jack?"

I could tell she was pissed behind her cautious question. My guitar teacher must have told her. Everyone knew everyone in the village. My mouth was full of cereal, so it bought me a few seconds. After I swallowed, I said, "I know lots of songs, Mom. It's all I need." A pang of guilt rode through my chest. I knew my mom had gone to a lot of trouble to get the guitar because I am left handed.

"Take a break for now, but keep the door open, Jack. Music is a skill you'll use all your life."

"Okay." I was relieved she didn't make a huge deal about it. She must have used up all her worry on Quinn.

I biked to school like usual, and Mom drove. She always stayed late at school to prepare her lessons, so I rode my bike to get back home earlier. In the winter, I sometimes had a ride from one of my friends' parents, or I walked. Nothing was too far in Lytton.

* * *

It was April Fool's Day at school. It mostly consisted of our teachers telling us goofy things that were obviously false. In gym class, our gym teacher made us run backward around the schoolyard. One kid tripped and tore his pants. Everyone laughed and I guess Rick felt like a jerk because he had us run the right way after that.

Us kids did stupid things too, like convince each other to look away at a fake spider or say someone had green hair while we stole their fries at lunch.

There was a club fair halfway through lunchtime. Tables lined the back wall of the gathering space. The first was a crafting club, the second was a science club and the third was a biodiversity club. I was surprised by the last one. What the heck were they getting at with biodiversity? The girl behind the table was Tess. I'd seen her around. She was cute.

"Hey," she said when I paused at her table.

"What's happening," I said, scanning the pamphlets on display.

"We're looking for new members," Tess said. "Interested?" It was odd to see a club fair in April, but back in September we were all learning online.

One of the pamphlets' covers said, *What is Biodiversity?* I took one and stuck it into my math textbook. "I'll think about it," I told her. I hated to admit that I had no idea what the club was about. I was not a joiner when it came to clubs, but I didn't tell her that. I didn't want her to think I was stupid. Overall, it was a fun day.

TUESDAY APRIL 6

two months, three weeks and two days before the wildfire

Mr. Marconi is a huge fan of the Blue Jays. He was pumped that morning because the Jays beat the Texas Rangers 6–2. More importantly, I liked Mr. Marconi because he let me use his high-backed teacher's chair a lot. Whoever got the top mark in class for an assignment got to use his chair that day.

Maybe I didn't read much, but I knew a good story when I heard one. I was also getting the hang of hammering out stories for assignments. It wasn't hard. I basically wrote the way I talked. He liked that. He said he didn't care much about grammar and especially not commas. "Remember, I hate commas," he'd said one day. "They're like road bumps on the page."

"Write like your house is on fire," he'd said another time. He basically meant that once you get an idea, write it down fast. He said he was interested in the content, not the form. We could improve in form later, he said, but it was more difficult to get a good story idea.

One of the ways Mr. Marconi taught us to make our stories better was in a lesson about tangible and intangible things. He said that tangible things are things we experience with our senses, and, usually, we can put a dollar value on them. They are concrete and we can easily add details like their colour and shape. Intangible things are things we can't put a dollar value on, and they don't have physical form. They're harder to describe. I always think about that when I write my school assignments now.

When I got my story back today about the Chinese railway workers, my mark at the top of the page was a big, red A. Our class went to the Chinese History Museum in Lytton a couple of weeks ago. There were around 6,500 Chinese Canadian rail workers installing track through the toughest sections of the B.C. mountains alongside far fewer white people. They were paid only a dollar a day, whereas white workers always got more. Plus, they had to do the most dangerous work, like use nitroglycerine explosives to break up rock.

My story's main character was a Chinese worker who photo-bombed the *Last Spike* photo. It was about something intangible: racism. In real life, you can barely see one Asian Canadian in the *Last Spike* photo. That was racist as heck.

My dad's grandfather was Asian, and he married a white woman. They lived in Vancouver. I think that makes me one-eighth Asian. Scott and Rory don't believe me. They say I don't look Asian so shut up about it. Even though my dad has way more European in him than Asian, he says, "It's good to be proud of all parts of your heritage." So I am.

* * *

It was dry and warm for April. After school, Scott, Rory and I went for a ride around the village in just our t-shirts and no jackets. It was 15 degrees. I loved spring in the Thompson-Nicola Valley because it was usually warm and sunny, although not usually this warm.

Our favourite place to go when we were young was onto the CN pedestrian bridge over the Fraser River. It was best when a train came, and sparks flew from the wheels in the half light at dusk. When we were younger, we'd get sticks and throw them through the grate into the river. Sometimes we spit if a boat was going by, but it was super hard to hit anything, and we never did, so we never got in trouble for it.

Later, back at home, Quinn had an exercise elastic shut into the basement door, and she was lunging into the kitchen with her arms, training for tree planting. Mom looked like she'd eaten a sour pickle while she cooked dinner. I had to laugh seeing Mom's face, and she got pretty mad at me, so I escaped to the basement to game, interrupting Quinn's workout on my way down.

SATURDAY APRIL 24

two months and five days before the wildfire

Even though it was a Saturday, I got up early to say goodbye to Quinn. She was leaving to go to tree-planting orientation in Pemberton. It was still a dry April, and they were getting started early, she said.

"Lucky you," I said, meaning she wouldn't be hounded by Mom and Dad anymore.

"I'm not sure about that," she said, hugging me tight. "Ride hard, Jackhammer." She kissed my cheek.

Quinn and I used to race on the trails. Trying to keep up with her made me a better and faster rider. But I was surprised by her other remark: she wasn't sure about her decision to go tree planting? I guess it would be hard work.

"Plant lots of trees," I encouraged her while she grabbed her stuff and headed outside.

Mom, Dad and I stood at the open front door and

watched Quinn load her duffle bag into her rusty blue Corolla. It started to drizzle, and I was glad that she wouldn't see my tears through her spotty windshield. She backed out of the driveway, and then she was gone.

I went back to bed for a while, but I couldn't sleep. There wasn't the usual happy feeling for a Saturday morning. Dad wasn't frying bacon, and Mom wasn't making coffee. Finally, I decided to get up.

I built myself a Dagwood sandwich to take for my bike ride. I have no idea who or what Dagwood is, but whenever Dad makes a sandwich with everything he can find in the fridge, he calls it that. Mine was a double-decker Dagwood, with ham, Swiss cheese, mustard, mayo and sliced pickle on multigrain bread for the bottom layer, and roasted turkey, cheddar, sliced tomato, lettuce, butter and Dijon mustard on the top section. I double wrapped it so it wouldn't leak in my backpack and added it to the bottle of water and apple I'd grabbed. The rain had stopped, and the ground was already dry.

I got my bike out of the shed and hopped on. I headed across Lytton past the Trans-Canada Highway to the hill beyond. I missed family rides. Even the rides my dad and I took had recently died out. But I was just as glad to get away on my own.

The trails snaked through the trees, and I took the westerly fork. I pedaled hard. My nose and lungs were full of fresh, green forest air. I pumped my pedals hard and my legs burned. It felt good. When I'd spent my energy, I found a place to stop.

Spring in the valley was green, but soon almost

everything would be brown and scorched. That was the way of the semi-arid interior of British Columbia. While I munched my sandwich, a delicious work of art, I heard a downy woodpecker tapping on a nearby tree. Then a robin carrying a twig paused to look at me. "Time to build a nest?" I smiled as it flew across the trail.

After I finished my sandwich, I rode back to the village. Downhill was always faster and thrilling, bumping over roots and ridges in the trail.

* * *

When I got back to the house, out of breath, Glenda, our next-door neighbour, was visiting my mom. They were having coffee. Glenda taught grade three at our school, and my mom taught grade four. Dad was nowhere to be seen. I chuckled inwardly. He wasn't a fan of Glenda. He said she talked too much. I grabbed a fresh-baked, apple-cinnamon muffin from the counter from the dozen Glenda had brought and headed downstairs.

Dad was watching the news on the family room TV while simultaneously scrolling through social media on his phone. I joined him on the sofa.

"Maybe next time you can come with me for a ride?" I asked.

"I'd love to, Son, if I'm not wiped from work."

TUESDAY MAY 11

one month, two weeks and four days before the wildfire

Rick Green was my photography teacher. He was young and cool and athletic. I often saw him running around the streets of the village. I guess he liked to stay in shape. He told us students to call him Rick, but we found it easier to call him by his first and last name together because there was another Rick in the village.

The first assignment he gave us was to take a portrait of the environment. "A portrait needs to do more than be a snapshot," Rick Green said. "It should show the land's personality. And once you've taken a photo you're happy with, write a short paragraph to describe it."

The class groaned collectively.

* * *

After school, I decided it was a perfect day to ride, and I pushed up my sleeves as I got onto my bike. I rode across the highway to Ponderosa Heights, to Rory's house.

"Let's do our photography assignment," I said when he opened his door. We rode over to Scott's place next. He lived right up beside the forest. The smell of pine was strong there with the sun heating the pine needles. We headed up an old logging road that snaked eastward.

That area had been logged a long time ago. Lodgepole pine trees had been planted and they were growing thick there. They were so straight and tall that it looked like a forest of telephone poles, to be honest. I snapped a few pictures of the new-growth forest on my new-old cell phone. I didn't have data on it, but I could use it with Wi-Fi to email Rick Green the photo for my assignment.

I hoped he'd like it. It felt eerie to me there, like a giant mountain lion was going to run out at us.

"Let's get out of here," I called to Scott and Rory. A shiver ran down my legs.

"Chicken! Squaaaak! Squaaak! Squaaak!" Scott mocked me.

"Shut up," Rory said. He was always protective of his brothers and me. Not that he needed to be, but it felt kind of good. Scott moved to Lytton two years ago and was still considered new by everyone who'd lived there longer. It felt like Scott was still trying to fit in with us, and Rory and I liked to make it awkward for him, even though we accepted him.

On the way back to Lytton, Rory and Scott stopped and took photos of random stuff, hoping something would be good enough for their assignment.

Back at home, I showed my photos to my dad. He works in forestry, so he knows lots about logging and reforestation.

"Nice looking trees," he said. "It's a stand of lodgepole pines."

"But all the same kind?" I asked.

"Forestry decides what the best type of tree is for the area based on soil, growing conditions and the types of trees that would be most hardy. Like farming wheat."

A thought struck me. "Will they be cut down again?" If trees were planted like farming and eventually harvested like wheat, then we wouldn't be mountain bike riding in the same forest anymore.

"It looks like they are approaching maturity," Dad said. "They'll be harvested in the near future."

I was ticked off. "It'll look terrible. Why do they have to ruin the forest?"

"We grow a lot of trees for pulp to make paper and lumber for here and other countries. Plus, it provides jobs."

I put my phone into my pocket and plopped down on the sofa. The forest was providing work for my dad and for Quinn, and it was providing people with the supplies they needed. Things weren't as simple as I'd like.

"Don't worry . . . the cutters leave a large buffer, not like the old days when they clear-cut everything."

I was glad then that Quinn was a tree planter. Her work was super important. She and the other tree planters made sure there were always lots of trees.

SUNDAY MAY 16

one month and thirteen days before the wildfire

It was early Sunday and still cool outside. It was going up to 29 degrees today, and I wanted to ride before the day heated up. I put my phone in my pocket for another photography assignment from Rick Green. We were supposed to take a photo of an animal.

I decided not to get Scott and Rory because it would take too long, and they would not be quiet enough for what I wanted to do. I rode across the CN pedestrian bridge and over the Fraser River. Then I followed Spencer Road to the Nikaia Creek trail, which snakes along the mountain toward Stein Valley Park.

It seemed like the whole world was pushing ahead, always turning, always changing. The seasons and days passed like the people along the Trans-Canada Highway, always rushing past Lytton on their way to somewhere else. And worst of all, the summers were getting hotter and dryer. I guess you could say I was rushing ahead, too, except the two wheels of my bike spun under me and took me where time seemed to stand still.

Once I got near a clearing, I saw the back end of a mountain lion rush into the brush. I didn't bother stopping since it was long gone. Farther up the trail, I saw a coyote out hunting, but when it saw me on my mountain bike it startled and took off. There was no way I had time to photograph it from astride my bike. I'd have to find a place to sit still and quiet.

I rode uphill to a higher elevation. My heart was beating like a freight train, and my lungs were yelling for air. I stopped and sat down on a stump. I gulped water from my bottle and looked back across the valley. I could see Lytton, but most of it was hidden behind a ridge and trees. I remembered when I stood at my kitchen window looking out toward the mountain. From that side, I could see the mountain through the trees. It was a weird feeling, thinking about the different perspectives.

While I sat on the stump and sipped water, my heart gradually slowed, and my lungs caught up with the air they needed. I breathed deeply and sat still, watching for an animal to stop hiding so I could take its photo. I got my phone ready and tried not to move.

The sun was high in the sky, and it warmed my bare arms and face. There was no shade next to the tree stumps and boulders. The short stubby grass and sagebrush released a tang into the air.

After a while, a jackrabbit hopped into the clearing. It

stopped for a few seconds. I held up my phone and clicked just in time before it took off, startled by my movements. When I looked at the photo, I thought it was great, even though it was slightly blurry. The hotter it got, the less of a chance there was of anything else coming out into the clearing. The longer I waited, the more it became clear that my first photo would have to do.

I sat for a while longer, enjoying the feeling that for a little while, everything stood still and perfect.

MONDAY JUNE 21

one week and a day before the wildfire

It was the last full week of school and the first National Indigenous Peoples Day. We had the day off. Rick Green had given us our last photo project for the school year. We had to take an action photo. *That will be easy*, I thought.

I rode over to Rory's place, and when he came out of his house and got on his bike, I snapped photos of him. He looked toward me and squinted. The sun was in his eyes, and at 35 degrees in the sun, he looked hot and sweaty. Even though it was blazing, we wore our helmets since we planned to do jumps on the trails.

After I snapped the photos, Rory said, "You dirtbag." But he was smiling and laughing at the same time, and I knew he didn't mean anything bad. He looked kind of proud.

"I took a picture of my mom. She's working on a craft," Rory said, pedaling hard beside me on the trail.

"Sick," I said, meaning that was great. I liked Rory's mom, Colleen. She was always nice to me. She had crafts for sale at the Klowa Art Café. She worked at Hans Knakst Tsitxw (Helping Hands) Society Reaching Out Centre. Sometimes after school Rory and I went there and took candies from the dish on the counter, and she let us. She was usually on the phone or talking to someone.

"I can't be gone long, Jack. We're driving to Kamloops for ceremonies today."

"Okay," I said. I knew the ceremonies were important to him.

* * *

Every summer for the past few years, we took shovels with us into the forest trails. We made ramps for jumps or repaired them. There were a lot of dead trees down in the natural forest, and we rode along dry creek beds, up and over banks, and jumped across sections where the rain washed away dirt from rocky ledges.

I was already thinking about what I'd write about Rory. I'd write that he was chill. He made jokes about everything. If I had a brother, I'd want him to be Rory. Rory had two younger brothers. They wrestled like crazy until their dad yelled at them to go outside, but they weren't angry when they wrestled.

Our photo projects were due by Thursday because Rick Green needed time to mark them and add them to our final grade. Finishing grade nine was a big deal for a lot of kids because it meant the end of middle school.

But for me, I was going to go to the same school, so it didn't matter much.

The trail was bone dry and I was glad. Riding in mud wasn't my favourite. If it happened, it happened, and it just meant a lot more clean up afterward. But it had barely rained all May and June, so there was no mud. Regardless, it was still hard going on a dry trail as we rode to the place where we'd built jumps every summer, out behind Skihist Provincial Park.

When we got to our jumps, we laughed and hollered while we took turns going over them. It was the best. I couldn't think of anything else I'd rather be doing.

At one point, I got off my bike and snapped photos of Rory in the air as he flew off the biggest jump. His hands gripped his handlebars, and he stuck his legs out at the sides, off his pegs. He looked cool.

"Yahoo!" he yelled while he was in the air.

Riding back to town was fast on the declining trail. I was hot and sweaty. After I left Rory at his house, I headed across the highway to the village.

There was a new sign at the end of a driveway. It said Tess's Trees. *Cool*, I thought, riding home. Tess sells trees. Even though there were lots of trees around Lytton, I could see that some people might want different kinds of trees to fill in empty spaces. She was all about biodiversity. It seemed like a nerdy thing to be into for such a pretty girl.

After I rinsed the dust off my bike with the hose, I stood in the shower for five minutes to cool off, lathering up with the peppermint shampoo. It was refreshing. Then I gamed in the basement for the rest of the day.

* * *

Before I shut off my bedroom light, I decided I should study math for the exam on Wednesday. It was hot outside still, and even the basement felt warm, so I only had a sheet as my cover. Tess's biodiversity club pamphlet slid out of my textbook onto my bed. I read it from front cover to back cover. I was struck by how heavily used areas and genetically modified plants, including trees, were not good for our environment. It reduced biodiversity and then the planet was less resilient.

The pamphlet quoted the federal government's target to safekeep biodiversity by preserving wild places or creating conservation areas out of 25 per cent of Canada's lands by 2025, 30 per cent by 2030 and 50 per cent by 2050. That sounded amazing. But what about forestry? Didn't we need to keep growing and selling trees for jobs?

I fell asleep without studying math, but I was good at math so it didn't matter. That night I dreamed about Tess. When I woke up in the morning, I had a hard time looking at myself in the mirror.

WEDNESDAY JUNE 23

seven days before the wildfire

Mr. Marconi was crabby because the Blue Jays were on a losing streak. They'd lost two games against Boston, plus two more against Tampa Bay. I liked seeing him this way. It felt more real than when a teacher tries to be fake nice all the time. He even yelled a little when his desk drawer wouldn't shut, but it wasn't directed at anyone.

I was getting sick of being at school knowing that summer holidays were coming. It was good that the school had air conditioning, or no one would have gone. Even with the A/C, the school felt stuffy and too warm while we had final exams.

* * *

After my math exam, I rode my bike home to find a stray dog hanging out in the yard. He didn't run away when I petted him. "Thirsty? Want some water?" He panted while his tongue hung out of his mouth.

I went into the house and filled a stainless-steel bowl with water. When I put it on the shady side of the front steps, the dog drank and drank until the bowl was almost empty. I filled it again and then held the door open and called to the dog to come inside. He followed me to the kitchen while I looked inside the fridge for something to eat. There was some old-looking lunch meat at the back of the meat and cheese drawer.

"Here you go, boy," I said. The dog almost snapped off my fingers when he snatched the ham from my hand.

He licked the ham juice off my fingers while I had a good look at him. "I haven't seen you around before." He was black and white, probably a border collie. I'd seen that kind of dog on TV. He followed me downstairs and had a nap in the cool family room while I gamed.

A while later, I heard Mom call that it was dinnertime. I went upstairs and the dog followed.

Mom had bought submarine sandwiches from the deli. "No dogs in the house!" she yelled when she spotted him. "Get it out of here!" She was afraid of dogs. One bit her when she was a kid.

"He's friendly. Look!" I petted his head and put my hand by his mouth. I laughed as I stood with my hand in the dog's mouth and drool ran over his lips and dripped onto the floor. I took my hand out and the dog licked it.

"I don't care. He goes. NOW." Mom took two cold pops out of the fridge and slammed the door. When my mom was like that, there was no reasoning with her. I took the dog outside.

The next morning, I took part of my leftover submarine sandwich outside to give to the dog for breakfast, but he was gone.

FRIDAY JUNE 25

five days before the wildfire

Mr. Marconi was pumped because the Blue Jays had won against Baltimore 9–0. They were on a winning streak, so Mr. Marconi had his wife bake cookies for everyone at school. He was creating a Blue Jays fan club. The cookies weren't bad. They had mini-M&Ms. I liked the ones my mom made better with full-sized M&Ms, but she doesn't bake them for everybody in the whole school. That would take a lot of M&Ms.

Usually, at the end of the school year, we go to the village pool for an afternoon, but it was closed for upgrades. That stunk big time. Mr. Marconi said to the class, "There's no point in doing any outdoor sports because Lytton is in a heat dome. It's setting another record high today at over thirty-nine degrees."

"What about the swimming hole?" I asked.

"No, it's dangerous," Mr. Marconi said, which wasn't true. Instead, he planned a Scrabble tournament. The only thing I hated more than the idea of a Scrabble tournament was the team crossword competition we would play the following week, on Monday and Tuesday, our last two days of school. Lots of kids said they planned to skip, but when your mom is a teacher, there's no skipping. She'd find me and make me go to school anyway, so why bother trying?

* * *

After school, Rory and I rode to the swimming hole. Scott couldn't come because he was starting a job at the deli washing dishes. Lame. His parents wanted him to start saving for his post-secondary education, he said. I was glad my parents hadn't started to pressure me about that yet. I knew it was coming soon since Quinn wasn't home.

Anyway, I knew why Mr. Marconi said the swimming hole was dangerous. At least one person drowned every year somewhere in B.C. There were tourists who went out river rafting and kayaking, and they sometimes capsized. If they had guides, the guides rescued them, but lots of people didn't hire guides. Besides, sometimes people party at the shore at night and get the bad idea to swim where it isn't safe. Rory and I were not that stupid. We only swam where it was safe.

At our swimming hole, the river dumped gravel out straight from one of the bends. The swimming hole formed between that gravel bar and the shore. Our hole was about two metres deep. It felt amazing on a hot day.

Rory and I still had our backpacks since we hadn't gone home after school. We dumped our bikes and backpacks on the shore, pulled off our t-shirts and ran straight into the water. We dunked our heads under and splashed around.

Rory said, "I'm never getting out."

The water was sweet relief and pockets where the water ran over the sun-warmed rocks were like sunspots. There was something about the taste of the water, the smell of sun-baked pine trees along the shore and kids yelling that felt like all the good things about summer.

I thought of Quinn planting trees somewhere in a remote area of B.C. *She must be suffering in the heat*, I thought. I hoped she had lots of water to drink. Maybe it wasn't as hot where she was. That thought made me feel better about her being out there somewhere.

Scott showed up when he finished his shift, and Tess showed up with her friends Kallie and Jaime. She looked so happy. I felt miserable.

The girls shrieked when they got into the water wearing t-shirts and shorts.

Suddenly, a train rattled close by over the train bridge, jolting me away from my thoughts. Its steel wheels sparked.

"Hey, how long can you hold your breath?" Rory asked.

"I have a waterproof watch," Jaime said. "Let's have a competition."

"I'm first!" yelled Kallie.

"Whatever," Scott said. "The girls can go first."

After all the girls had a turn, then Scott, it was my turn. My time was good, but not the best.

"Rory had the best time," Jaime announced at the end.

I was surprised, since I have better lungs when we ride bikes. I wasn't called the Jackhammer for no reason.

"Loser!" I banged into Rory and pushed him under the water.

He jumped up from the water and grabbed me, pushing me under. I held my breath until my brain screamed for air. Then I popped up out of the water.

Tess was next to us, pushing Rory away from me. "Don't be a bully!" she yelled.

"We're just fooling around," I told her. "Want a boost?" When Quinn and I were young, we took turns stepping into each other's cupped hands and we'd boost the other up and over our shoulder to dive into the water.

Tess looked at my interlocked fingers and she knew what I meant. She put her small foot into my hands and put pressure on them as she gripped my shoulders. I bent my knees to get more leverage, and I hoisted her up and over my left shoulder. I felt a release of pressure as she dove into the water behind me.

I turned and saw her pop up right away. She laughed and brushed her hands through her wet hair.

When Kallie and Jaime saw what we'd done, they bugged Scott and Rory to give them boosts too, and Tess took a few more dives with me. We grinned and laughed. Rory boosted Kallie a few times and they had a great time, but Jaime was annoyed since Scott wasn't as strong and couldn't boost her as high, so she got Rory to boost her, too. Scott looked dejected as he got out of the water and sat on the shore.

After a while, the rest of us got out of the water to sit on the shore with Scott. I'd started to get hungry, so I emptied my backpack onto the gravel.

"Snacks," I said. "This is what happens when your mom is a teacher." There were two apples, three granola bars and two small packages of mini-Oreo cookies. I could smell a barbecue going somewhere in Lytton, and I knew it was time to go home for supper soon, too, but not yet. It was still too hot. And besides, it was Friday night, so there was no school until Monday.

"Dibs on the chocolate," Tess said, taking a granola bar and apple.

Rory added Cheetos and Glossette Raisins to the snack pile from his backpack. Everyone dug in. I grabbed the last thing left: a bruised apple.

"Hey, I read your club pamphlet," I said to Tess. "Do you think we can actually help change things?"

"Don't get her started," Kallie said, covering Tess's mouth with her hands.

Tess pulled Kallie's hands down. "I think it's worth a fight." Kallie took a more aggressive hold over Tess's mouth, and she and Tess laughed so hard that they fell back and rolled around. It must have felt pokey on the gravel.

After Tess freed herself from Kallie, she continued. "I don't think most people care about this stuff, but our planet depends on us."

I looked at her sitting beside me. "You're right. It does matter."

"Cool," she said. "So you're joining?"

I laughed like a dork. "To do what?" I forced my face to stop smiling.

"I need help with computer stuff." She finished the granola bar and bit into the apple. After she swallowed, she said, "You like computer class, don't you?"

I didn't mind computer class. "It's okay." What kid wouldn't? It was a change from listening to teachers talk. I didn't mind building websites and creating graphic art. "Maybe..." my voice trailed off. "I'll think about it." I wanted to be near her, but I felt a pull to be uncommitted to a boring club when I could be out riding my bike.

All the snacks were gone. Tess, Kallie and Jaime got ready to leave.

"See you later," I said to Tess. She looked back and smiled.

Rory, Scott and I sat on the shore looking at the water and the sunset. The air cooled and mist rose over the water, the scent of black cottonwood and damp soil drifted like napalm. An elk with giant antlers came out of the trees far down the river. It scanned right and left. Soon after, a female elk from the woods joined the male. She lapped water. My heartbeat felt like the rainless thunder of a summer night.

SATURDAY JUNE 26

four days before the wildfire

Rory came over and we planned to bike to the deli to bug Scott. We had the swimming hole, but the pool was really fun, too. I felt deflated that it was still closed for upgrades, and I didn't know when I'd start my summer job. I'd worked at the pool last summer doing clean up. It wasn't too bad.

"Don't ride in the forest in this heat," Dad said. He munched cold cereal. "There's a lot of tinder and anything could spark a fire. There's a fire ban, too, so no campfires are allowed."

"Sure, whatever," I said. "We're going to the deli."

"It's supposed to get up to forty-four degrees today," Mom said. "Unbelievable. Make sure you fill your water bottles before you go out, and wear helmets."

"It's too hot," I said. "It's cooler without helmets."

"Stay in the village," Dad said. "Okay?"

I felt like I was five years old and grounded.

"Yeah, sure. Whatever." Outside, the heat thumped down on us. I wouldn't have bothered going out at all except I wanted to get junk food at Super Foods for us before we hid in the basement to game. And maybe we'd go swimming again later. Maybe I'd see Tess.

* * *

On 4th Street, a market was set up with tables and shade tents. I spotted Rory's mom, Colleen, selling her crafts at one of the tables, and then I saw Tess.

"Hey, let's see what they've got," I said.

"They're closing the market early today," Colleen said when we got to her table. The shade felt good under her awning. But even in the shade, everyone was sweating. "It's too hot. You boys should get out of this heat," Colleen added. "Here." She passed Rory a handful of coins. "Get some cold drinks."

"Thanks." Rory hugged his mom.

"Sweet," I said and smiled at her.

A couple tables down, Tess and her friends were handing out her club pamphlets. Tess waved. *Her club wasn't just a school thing*, I thought.

"Hey." It was the first time I'd seen Tess outside of school and away from the river. I didn't know what to say.

Colleen broke the awkward pause. "You boys find some place to cool off, okay?" She packed her crafts into a bin.

"We'll get that," Rory said. He picked up one side of the massive bin, and I took hold of the other.

"See you later," I called over my shoulder, but there was no reply. Tess probably didn't know I was even talking to her.

We carried the bin to Colleen's minivan on the street.

"Come on," Rory said after. "Let's bug Scott." We pushed our bikes down the street a bit to the Lyl' Towne Deli and Sandwich Shop.

"Hey, you animal," Rory said to Scott who was behind the counter.

"I'll take an orange Gatorade," I said. There were lots of flavours of drinks, and they looked cold inside the cooler. "And a slice of pepperoni pizza." I couldn't remember the last time I'd had pizza.

"Green Gatorade for me, and the same for pizza," Rory said.

We drank our Gatorades, and then we put our coin cash into the empty bottles for Scott to fish out.

"You guys are brutal," Scott complained.

Considering it was supposed to be air conditioned in the deli, it didn't seem so cool. I was sweating like crazy and sweat ran down Scott's face at the counter. He took the bottles to the kitchen and washed them out at the sink so he could get the money for our purchases.

Rory and I laughed as we sat down at one of the tables to wait for our pizza. We didn't smell so good. Our t-shirts had sweat circles at our armpits and necklines.

"My dad said we're leaving after school to visit my cousins in Kamloops."

"That sucks," I said. Canada Day would be boring without him.

"I'm gonna be in a drum circle," he said. His face was

serious but proud. "It will be a healing ceremony."

"Sucks so bad, what happened," I told him. Unmarked graves and burned churches were in the news every day.

"It's an honour to drum," Rory said. "I'm kind of excited about it."

"Get someone to take pictures," I said. I thought about how cool he would look drumming. It would make an awesome portrait.

We ate our pizza in silence. My throat felt dry and closed and I forced my pizza down. Finally, we were ready to go.

"See you at my place," I told Scott. "Bring a controller."

"Later," he said over his shoulder. He looked disappointed that he had to work and we didn't.

Outside, I saw the stray border collie trotting along the street. I tried to bike after it, but it went down an alley and disappeared.

"Where are you going?" Rory sounded annoyed, so I gave up. I knew the village dog would be okay. He was resourceful. He must have someone else to take care of him.

SUNDAY JUNE 27

three days before the wildfire

Scott and Rory went home late last night. I slept in the basement on the sofa. Mom and Dad slept in Quinn's room.

"It's too hot," Mom said, coming out of Quinn's bedroom. "It's going up to forty-six degrees today. I can't believe it. I can't stand this heat much longer." She headed upstairs.

"Quinn phoned last night," Dad said to me, heading to the stairs too. "She's doing well."

"Why didn't you get me?" I was ticked. I hadn't talked to her since she'd left. I missed her. Without Quinn around, Mom and Dad had no one to pick on except me.

"You were busy gaming with Scott and Rory," Dad said.

"What did she say?" I followed him up the stairs.

"She's sore." Dad plopped down at the table and scrolled through the social media feed on his phone. "But she's making lots of money."

"She'd better save, because she'll need it for school," Mom said, still not giving up hope that Quinn would decide on a profession other than tree planting. She was making iced coffees at the counter. "Want one?" she asked me.

The cold coffee, cream and ice all looked good in the blender cup. "Put sugar in mine." We didn't have a Tim Hortons in Lytton, but I'd had iced cappuccinos from the one in Lillooet. My dad worked out of the forestry office there.

"Can we go to Lillooet today? For something to do?"

"You guys need to do your laundry today. I want to leave for Victoria after school is finished. It's too hot in this valley."

I hated visiting my aunt and cousins in Victoria. They were three-year-old twins, always screaming and making big messes. "Can't I stay home?" I begged. "I'm old enough." I wanted to hang out with my friends. Maybe even Tess. I knew where her place was, along the highway. I could bike there.

"No." Mom turned on the blender. It screamed and rattled while it crushed the ice and blended the coffee. My ears hurt. When the horrible noise ended, she poured the coffee into three glasses and handed one to me. It tasted cold and sweet.

"You can stay home when you have your own car," Dad said. "You need to be able to get around better."

"I can get around fine," I said. "I have my bike, and I still have my old skateboard." I used to skateboard around the pavement in the village, and I'd jump off the stairs that went up the hill by the Village Hall.

"No," Mom repeated, seemingly unmoveable. But I'd

45

learned over the years that persistence paid off, so I kept the pressure on.

"I can save for my own car when the pool rehires me." It was two years until I could get my driver's licence. That would mean two summers to save for a car. There were so many cool biking trails within a short driving distance. I imagined that I would be gone all the time riding. I wondered if Tess liked to ride.

Dad stopped scrolling on his phone and looked up. "Not a bad idea. Start looking through used car ads. That way you'll know how much to save."

"Don't encourage him, Rob," Mom said, a look of fear in her eyes. "He's coming to Victoria. His aunt and cousins want to see him." She knew her position was slipping. If Dad was on my side, I had a chance.

"The pool will hire me again, once they're open." I spent all the cash I'd made last summer on junk food and my Xbox and games. This time, I would be smarter. I'd save most of my money.

"He should work and save if he can get a job," Dad said. "He's almost fifteen."

"Nobody cares what I think," Mom said in a huff.

"I can't go either," Dad said. "Sorry, Cindy. I can't take any time off this summer. With this heat dome, we're slammed with forest fires. I'm organizing the fire crews." Dad had to be at the worst hot spots in the forests. They used helicopters to survey the fires, and Dad would direct them to the worst ones, especially the ones that were headed toward populated areas.

I figured it wouldn't hurt to push my point one last time.

"I can work at the pool when it reopens, and when it's too hot, I'll stay in the basement out of the heat. I promise I won't mountain bike in the forest until after it rains."

"This could be a good opportunity for Jack to practice being responsible for himself." Dad winked at me. "What do you think, Cindy? We want to be empty nesters one day."

Mom, enjoying her leverage, sipped her iced coffee and searched my face for signs of responsibility. I couldn't blame her for being skeptical. I hadn't shown much initiative. I decided I needed to put more effort in around the house to prove I could take care of myself.

"Let me think about it overnight. In the meantime, you have got to do your laundry! I can smell it from here."

I could see my pile of dirty clothes from the kitchen, too. "You're right." I'd worked through all my t-shirts and shorts during the hot weather. It all stunk like a garbage heap. "I'll do it now."

"Who is going to buy and prepare food for him while I'm away, Rob?" Mom started in on Dad.

"We can figure it out." Dad scrolled through his feed. "I ate cereal and sandwiches when my folks left me at home at his age."

I hopped up from the table and took my clothes to the basement laundry room. I shoved in as much clothing as would fit. I could hear Mom working on Dad upstairs.

"It's not as safe now as it was then, Rob." Her voice grew louder and louder. I poured lots of liquid laundry soap on top of my clothes, closed the lid and pressed start.

MONDAY JUNE 28

two days before the wildfire

There were only two more days of school before summer break. I slept late and, in a daze, found an old green t-shirt to wear. It had a hole in it, but it would work. I didn't have time for breakfast, so Mom stuffed two protein bars and an apple into my backpack. I remembered about my laundry, so I ran downstairs to put it in the dryer, but when I opened the washer lid, there were a lot of suds. "Dang."

I turned the washer to "Rinse" and pressed start before I ran back upstairs. Mom and I rushed outside. She got into her car to drive to school, and I hopped on my bike, even though I knew I'd be late. Mom didn't bother nagging me about being late because she knew the other teachers would give me detention if I did it too often. She'd said I was old enough to get myself to school and be responsible for any consequences that came my way from being late.

Mr. Marconi didn't give me heck for being late that day. He was pumped because the Blue Jays won three of their four games against Baltimore. *Thank you, Jays*, I thought, smiling.

Judging by the empty seats, it looked like lots of kids had skipped. We waited a while longer, and a few more kids trickled into class. Then he got us started on the team crossword puzzle challenge. And because Mr. Marconi was so cheerful, we convinced him to let us use dictionaries.

"Consider all the possibilities," he said. "That's how you'll win." Then he added, "The losing teams have to clean the classroom today and tomorrow."

Everyone groaned. "There's so much junk! What do we do with it?" one of the girls said.

"Don't worry. I'll give you instructions. Now, for the crossword challenge, I've used words from all your reading and vocabulary lists this semester."

I thought back to the books we'd read.

I liked teams because we fed off each other's ideas. Someone called out a word and we tried it in the squares on the whiteboard. If it didn't work, someone else would come up with something. I liked it better than working alone on this stuff.

As the game wore on, I actually got a few of the words right. My team passed through to the finals to be held on Tuesday, the last day of school.

Rory and Scott were both on losing teams, so they pretended to clean the classroom while they made jokes and the girls did the work.

* * *

After school, Rory had to watch his little brothers until his mom got home from work. "I'm going over to Rory's," I said.

"Lytton set another heat record today. Remember what your dad said. Don't ride bikes in the forest. It's too dry. Anything could start a fire."

"I'm not five years old," I groaned.

"The pool called. They want you to work there again this summer when they open." I didn't have my own cell number, and with everyone knowing everyone in the village, it wasn't unusual to have my mom convey messages to me.

"Can I stay, then?" Biking, hanging out at the swimming hole without a curfew — it was all in sight.

"I told the pool *yes* on your behalf. I have it all worked out. Your dad will come home as often as possible, and I talked with Glenda next door. I've given her money to take care of dinner for you every day while I'm away. She'll prepare food some days, but I told her it's okay to buy dinner when it's too hot to cook. I'll stock up on groceries before I leave so you can feed yourself breakfast and lunch. Plus, there's some cash for milk and fresh fruit in this drawer." She pulled the junk drawer open and showed me a baggie with a handful of loonies and toonies.

"You're the best." I hugged my mom. She felt small in my arms. When had she shrunk?

"Stop. You're making me hotter," she complained. "I can't believe you'd rather stay in this forty-six-degree sauna. Soak your t-shirt before you go outside. It will make the heat tolerable."

50

"Great idea." Now that Mom had agreed for me to stay in Lytton, my world felt perfect. No long drive across Vancouver. No long ferry ride across Georgia Strait. No long drive in Victoria traffic to my aunt's house. And best of all, no bratty cousins to put up with for weeks.

It felt like I had ridden to the peak of a mountain, and nothing was impossible for me now. I imagined that this was what it felt like to be an adult. They could decide to do whatever made them happy. They didn't have to listen to anyone.

I pulled my t-shirt off and Mom grabbed it from me. She held it under the kitchen tap while the cold water soaked it, then she wrung it out and handed it back to me. It felt freezing cold when I pulled it on over my head. My skin bristled under it.

"Here, wipe your face." Mom handed me a soaking-wet wash cloth. I opened it onto my hands and scrubbed my face with it. It felt cold and amazing. I kissed my mom's cheek.

"Thanks, Mom!" The kiss felt a little weird for the first time ever. I used to kiss my mom a lot when I was little, but I hadn't done it in a while. I guess I was excited about staying home and about her trusting me. Maybe I wouldn't do that again. Tess came to mind, and I tried to hide my feelings by turning my back to my mom.

Outside, the sun's ruthless heat pressed down on me, but the wet shirt helped. I hopped on my bike and pulled on my helmet since I had to ride across the Trans-Canada Highway.

The breeze was anything but refreshing as it carried

forest fire smoke throughout Lytton. It even dried my shirt by the time I made it to the highway. I stood astride my bike, waiting to cross while vehicles passed. My nose stung from the stink of hot rubber tires and tar-pitched asphalt. A tan pick-up truck streaked past with the windows down and loud music playing. The driver flicked a cigarette butt out of the window. It bounced along the asphalt until another vehicle, coming from the opposite direction, drove over it.

"Lucky." I shook my head. "He almost started a fire." Anger bubbled up inside me. Here I was, banned from riding the forest trails and turkeys like that driver could start a fire and not even know it. Didn't he know it was tinder dry all over the interior of B.C.? Didn't he know a fire could start with just one spark? My good mood had evaporated like the water in my t-shirt.

At Rory's we watched cartoons in the basement with his little brothers. There was a *SpongeBob SquarePants* marathon playing, so we watched about half a dozen episodes. The shows were funny, but what I enjoyed the most was watching Rory's little brothers squeal and laugh. Then Rory got us all multi-coloured space popsicles from the freezer. The blueberry, lime and cherry flavours zinged on my tongue. The little boys got it all over their faces and t-shirts. Rory had to wrestle them one by one on the carpet to clean them up before his mom got home.

A while later, when Colleen finally came home, Rory and I decided to bike down to the swimming hole.

"Be back before dark," Colleen said. "You have school tomorrow."

"Yeah, but it's the last day," Rory said. "We're not doing anything, anyway."

"Don't be late." Colleen put pizza pops into the microwave for dinner. When it dinged, she opened the door and transferred the hot food onto plates. She and Rory's brothers went downstairs into the basement family room to eat. Rory and I made peanut butter and raspberry jam sandwiches and filled water bottles so we could stay out late by the river. I hoped Tess would be there.

* * *

At the swimming hole, a group of tourists had a small campfire where they were roasting hot dogs. The hot dogs smelled good.

Rory and I dumped our bikes and the backpack on the gravel shore and ran into the water to cool off. I kept on my green t-shirt to let it get washed in the river. The hole by the hem was getting larger. Scott came from work and ran into the water, too.

"Hey, you guys want hot dogs?" a tourist called. "We have lots."

"Sure," I said. It sounded more appetizing than sandwiches. We got out of the water and went over to them. I didn't say anything about their fire, even though I knew there was a fire ban. The forest fire smoke was thick, so I didn't think anyone would have noticed this. Besides, it was a small fire, and it was right next to the river. It looked safe.

Rory, Scott and I ate two hot dogs each, then they gave us colas out of their blue Arctic cooler. There were two guys and three girls. They were laughing and joking. They poured something extra into their pop cans, but they didn't offer any to us. They were probably staying at one of the hotels right next to the river.

"Hey, I get to work at my dad's gas station this summer, when I get back from Kamloops," Rory said.

"That's epic. The pool called so I'm working there again," I said.

"Look at you guys, being all responsible," Scott laughed. He punched me lightly in the side.

I punched him back a little harder. "Dork."

We hung out for a while and watched the sun go down behind the mountains. I wished that Tess had come down to the river. Maybe once school was out, I could bike over to her place. I felt tense thinking about it, but if I didn't go, I might not get to see her all summer and I didn't want that.

"It's getting late," Rory said. "I have to go."

"Yeah, me too," Scott said, picking up his bike from the gravelly shore.

"Thanks for the hot dogs!" Rory called. The tourists all waved to us as we left.

When I looked back, the sparks from the fire rose in squiggly patterns over the river. It looked safe enough to me. The wind was blowing in the right direction away from Lytton. We rode back into the village where Scott and I went home one way, and Rory headed across the highway to his house.

I decided to sleep downstairs again because the house was like an oven. Even downstairs was uncomfortable. I tried one side, then the other. Plus, I was thinking about how I could talk to Tess and what I would say. I'd ask her for her phone number soon. I still didn't have data on my phone, but once I got working, I could get a data plan for it so I could text her.

TUESDAY JUNE 29

one day before the wildfire

It was the last day of school before summer holidays. I picked up my red t-shirt from the floor and put it on. In the kitchen, I held in my excitement about staying home so my mom wouldn't change her mind. If I was too excited, she'd get suspicious and think I would get up to all kinds of bad things if I acted like I'd rather have her away.

"Today is going to be another scorcher," Mom said. She pulled the milk out of the fridge for me and left it on the counter next to the box of cereal. The window was closed because Mom thought it kept the house cooler.

I breathed deeply to act calm. Through the window I could barely see the mountains across the river because of all the forest fire smoke. It was so ordinary to see smoke in the sky now that it didn't register in my brain that anything was abnormal.

"Why would you want to stay here?" Mom scowled. "Don't answer that. I know your cousins can be annoying, but it's cooler in Victoria."

"I like my job," I said. "I'll save money." *Best to appeal to her frugal side*, I thought, and not mention my plans to hang out with Tess and the guys as much as possible.

I poured cereal into a bowl and soaked it with cold milk. I decided to eat quickly over the counter because it was almost time to leave.

Mom put away the milk and put two energy bars and an apple into my backpack. I remembered my laundry and smelled my armpit to see how bad my t-shirt stunk. It was nasty and had a hole the size of a grapefruit, so I ran downstairs and pulled my still wet yellow t-shirt out of the washing machine and put it on. It felt cold. What a relief.

* * *

In English class, my team was disqualified by mid-morning. I was pretty happy because I was tired of doing crossword puzzles. It looked like Rory and Scott were having more fun cleaning the classroom with the girls.

While everyone helped clean or worked on the last crossword puzzle, Mr. Marconi went around and kept everyone on track, and he went through papers on his desk. He had a big stack he was working on when I decided to talk to him.

"I hope you're my English teacher next year," I said sheepishly. I wasn't used to saying nice things to people. Things were sort of backward with Rory and Scott because we said mean things to each other, but what we really meant is that we liked each other. It was our way.

Mr. Marconi smiled. "I hope you have a great summer, Jack. You've done great work this year."

It felt really good to hear him say that. My hard work had paid off. I guess he inspired me to care about my work. I could thank him for that. "Thanks." I left off the ending, *for your help.* The words got stuck in my throat. I left him at his desk to finish sorting his papers.

When it was time to go, he shook hands with each of us as we passed through the classroom door. He said, "Never give up, work hard," like we were going to the Olympics or something.

"I hope the Blue Jays win the World Series," I said. I meant that he was one of my best teachers ever.

* * *

Later, Rick Green gave us back our assignments. I got good marks on all of them.

"I have one final assignment for all of you over the summer," he said. He got up from his desk. "Whenever you see anything that is a good portrait, snap a photo. It could be a person, a place, an animal, an object, whatever."

"Do we get credit next year?" someone asked.

"Yes, I can give you a mark for it in the fall," Rick Green said. "Mainly, the benefit will be that you'll find you look at the world in a different way."

Next, we had to prepare to leave for the summer break by cleaning the shelves and desks and taking out the trash.

"It's been a good semester." Rick Green smiled. "I'll see you all in the fall. I can't wait to see all your photos."

"Cool, thanks," I said. I hoped he knew how much I liked his class. Even though I was looking forward to summer, I was kind of already looking forward to his photography class again in the fall. I wondered what kind of assignments he'd have for us.

* * *

"Today was another record temperature at almost forty-nine degrees," Mom said after school. "I still think you should come to Victoria with me. It's so much cooler by the ocean."

"I can't. My job starts soon," I said. Scott was off work today, so he'd come home with me. Rory and his family had left right after school to drive to Kamloops, so he couldn't come. I thought about how he would be in a drumming circle. He must have been really excited. I wished I could see him there. I'd take photos of him and his family. Colleen would probably take her handmade crafts.

"Allegedly," Mom said, defeated.

What did she mean, allegedly? I tried to act casual, focusing on the water bottle that I held under the tap. Next, I shoved some ice cubes in. Even though I was trying to act cool, I felt beads of sweat trail down my neck and back.

"I hope you have a safe journey," Scott said. He filled a water bottle with ice first, then pushed me aside to hold it under the tap.

"Thanks, Scott." Mom smiled at him, and she elbowed me. "Why can't you be polite, Jack?"

Scott burst out laughing while I pushed him.

""Shut up, dork," I said.

He ran down the stairs ahead of me, eager to game. It didn't look like we would be going swimming. I wondered if Tess would be at the swimming hole with her friends, and I would miss out on seeing her. I hadn't seen her at school. I wondered, had she and her family left on a trip? I didn't know when I'd get to see her again. The whole summer stretched out in front of me, but suddenly I felt down about it. It would be a repeat of last summer unless Tess was going to be in Lytton.

I remembered how serious she was about trees and biodiversity. How was it possible that she cared so much about such a serious topic while me and my friends gamed? I'd never be good enough for her. I vowed to talk to her about her club. But for tonight, I was going to thrash Scott in the game.

WEDNESDAY JUNE 30

the day of the wildfire

Mom banged around upstairs while she got ready to leave on her trip to Victoria. I think she was extra loud on purpose, so I'd wake up.

I groaned. My head was full of video games and Tess. I'd slept in my shorts again, so I didn't have to think about what to wear for bottoms, but then I remembered my clothes in the washer, so I went to get another t-shirt. When I opened the lid, the clothes stunk. I went upstairs from the cool basement not bothering to put on a shirt. How was I supposed to prove to Mom that I could be responsible if I couldn't even wash my own clothes? I decided I'd rewash them later. Mom would be gone for weeks, so she wouldn't know.

The house was hot and stuffy. Mom was wearing shorts and a tank top, and she had her shoulder-length black hair pulled into a ponytail. It was odd to see her like that. She swiped at her forehead with her arm, and it made her bangs stick up funny.

"Check to make sure all the appliances are off before you go out," she said. "Always lock the door. Lots of tourists stop in Lytton in the summer and you never know if someone will snoop around. Don't let that stray dog into the house. It might poop on the floor."

"You worry too much."

"I don't have a good feeling about this."

She can't change her mind now, I worried. "It'll be okay."

She packed a compact insulated lunch bag with sandwiches for her drive. "I gave Glenda the code for the door so she can check on things."

"You don't trust me." I rubbed sleep from my eyes.

"You're only fourteen years old, and your dad is away at a forest fire. Check in with Glenda if you're going anywhere, please. For my peace of mind."

"I'm almost fifteen." Her worry was worse than usual.

"I can't believe I agreed to this. That's the least you can do. I don't want the house to burn down because you forgot to turn something off."

I sat at the table, waiting for this goodbye to be over. I didn't feel good that she didn't fully trust me, but it *was* my first time staying home alone. I felt excited to hang out with my friends and to hang out at the river as late as I wanted, so I promised myself that I wouldn't mess this up. I wanted her to trust me.

"I'll be responsible, Mom. Don't worry."

Mom hugged me extra hard. It felt weird since I was

so much taller than her. She pulled me tight and pressed her head against my collarbone. I arched my back a little away from her. When it finally ended, she ran out the door, started her car and gunned the engine. She kept the windows up as she drove off.

The stray dog was hanging out by a tree. I went to fill his water bowl, then called him to come inside as I went back to sleep in the basement for a while. It was too early to start the day for the first day of summer holidays.

* * *

I got up at noon and had cereal. I gave some to the dog, too, with milk and everything. Then I decided to ride down to the swimming hole, with no shirt and no helmet. It was hotter than a pizza oven. Outside, I saw Glenda watching me through her window. I waved.

The wind dried my sweat as it poured from me. The dog trotted next to my bike, then he laid down by the trees. I was excited that I might see Tess.

It felt great to be on summer break and I didn't want this summer to be the exact same as last summer, so I had to make sure to stir things up with Scott and Rory and Tess. I had to think of exciting things to do. But what? It was finally sinking in that I didn't have school for two whole months.

I got into the water to cool off, but no one showed up to join me, so I went and sat on shore by the dog and petted him. He seemed to relate to my feeling of anticipation since he kept sweeping the surroundings with his eyes, watching for movement. *I should leave*, I thought. *No, I should stay*, I battled myself.

After what felt like the end of an offensive on a war-torn beach, a bunch of kids turned up. *Tess.*

"Hey," I said to her, smiling.

"Hey," she smiled back. She turned and talked to her friends while they got into the water. I wanted her to talk to me, and I hated myself. I was too awkward.

I didn't know how to replicate the first time we swam together. I decided to float on my back and paddle around Tess and her friends, waiting to see if they would talk to me, or include me in whatever they were doing. They didn't.

We all swam for a while, close to each other. No one talked to me. The others got out and sat on shore. It was hot and smoky from the fires. The air felt restless, like something was going to happen, but I couldn't make myself do what I really wanted to do. Talk to Tess. I felt like a prisoner inside my body.

Suddenly, she said, "See you." And she smiled at me.

"Yeah, see ya later," I smiled. I guessed that this was awkward for her, too.

But when I headed home, I was feeling anxious and deflated again, not knowing when I would see her next. The dog came with me. He probably felt sorry for me.

* * *

Scott was coming over to game in the afternoon, so before he arrived, I had a long cool shower. I used the soap Quinn made, and I washed my hair with the peppermint shampoo. It reminded me of her. I was glad she was doing what she wanted to do. I suddenly felt alone. Mom and Dad were gone and Quinn was gone, too, so she couldn't encourage me by calling me the Jackhammer. I got out and put my dirty shorts back on. Then I remembered my clothes and pulled a wet red shirt from the washer. It didn't smell too bad on its own. I added more soap to the stinky clothes in the washer and turned it on again. I decided to play keep away with the dog until Scott turned up.

The dog whined and sat at the door. I pushed the door open for him and he went out while Scott came in. I watched the dog for a minute, walking away into the forest fire smoke and the crushing heat of the day. *He'll come back if he wants something*, I thought.

Scott brought orange Gatorade and day-old pizza from the deli.

"Hey, let's have iced coffee," I offered.

"Dude. That sounds great," Scott said.

First, I made double-strong coffee using the coffee maker. Then I crushed ice in the blender and added a ton of sugar and cream before I added the coffee. We carried our drinks and the pizza down to the basement with us.

Hours later, the floorboards creaked above our heads. *It must be Glenda coming into the house*, I thought.

She hollered down the stairs, "I brought you supper."

I went upstairs to see what it was. Scott followed me. She'd brought two homemade cheeseburgers with potato chips on the side. "Cool, thanks," I said.

Glenda transferred the food from her tray onto plates from the cupboard.

"Thanks!" Scott called as we returned to the basement with the food.

"Let me know if you need anything else, okay?" Glenda's voice followed us down the stairs. I could hear the door slam shut as she left.

Scott and I wolfed down the food. It was good Glenda had brought supper. I wasn't much of a cook. I put on a movie. It felt good to know there were no more school assignments to think about for months.

A while later, I heard Glenda come into the house again. Now what? I thought. I was a little hungry still. Maybe she'd brought dessert?

"GET UP HERE," she yelled. "NOW! HURRY!"

"What?" I said to Scott. "Did I leave the coffee maker on?" I yelled back at her.

I ran up the stairs. Scott followed. My heart pounded like a locomotive. The house was full of smoke. Angry flames roiled, consuming the house. Thoughts came like fragments of movies and games. We were under attack, I thought. I half expected military guys to jump out from the flames with submachine guns, but this was no game.

"JACK! THE HOUSE IS ON FIRE! GET OUT!" Glenda yelled.

"What's happening?" Scott stumbled into me as he emerged from the basement.

"Outside, NOW!" Glenda yelled.

Did I leave the coffee maker on when I made iced coffees? Did I forget to turn something off? This was the first time I'd been allowed to stay at home while Mom and Dad and Quinn were all away. This couldn't be happening. This was the first day of summer holidays. This was all my fault. I must have done something wrong.

I coughed and coughed. My lungs sucked the dirty air. My eyes and throat burned. I could hardly see the door through the smoke. I ran my hands along the hallway wall, feeling my way to the door. The door was open, and I rushed toward it. I turned back to look for my friend.

"Scott! Where are you?" I couldn't see him.

Suddenly, Scott rushed past me. Both of us raced down the wooden stoop to the front yard. The brittle lawn stabbed my bare feet, and I stared at the house. Flames jumped along the roof. The trees next to us were like tiki torches.

"My shoes! My shoes! I need my runners!" I rushed back inside the house, and Scott followed. Right inside the door, I looked down at the linoleum. I saw my shoes, so I picked them up and stopped, staring at the red-hot orange flames. Scott grabbed his shoes, too, and we were mesmerized. Frozen in a bizarre scene. Fear gripped me, and I couldn't move.

"GET OUT. NOW!" Glenda yelled into the house. "THE HOUSE IS ON FIRE!"

I coughed painfully, and my stinging eyes watered. I ran outside. The backyard and fence were on fire. Flames licked the back of the house. Glenda's house was on fire, too. Scott was beside me. Wind whipped the flames from treetop to treetop and from house to house. Ash and sparks fell like heavy rain. I saw the stray dog run down the road. I coughed and coughed. My throat burned.

"HURRY!" Glenda yelled from beside her car. "GET IN!" Her voice was full of panic, her eyes as large as Frisbees.

We ran for Glenda's car. I got in the front next to Glenda,

and Scott got into the backseat. Flames danced on rooftops and consumed buildings before our eyes.

"The shingles are burning!" Glenda cried.

"DRIVE!" Scott yelled. His voice shrill. "GO. GO. GO."

Glenda's hands shook. "OH NO, OH NO, OH NO! WHAT IS HAPPENING."

The car choked and buckled. It didn't want to start. Glenda rattled the key in the ignition and turned it back and forth. She pumped the gas pedal and tried again. It gurgled and choked.

"It's FLOODED!" Glenda shook all over.

"Try AGAIN." I yelled. I wished I had my licence.

The engine whirred and whirred. Finally, after what felt like forever, it started.

A fire engine flew past on another road, its siren screaming.

Glenda's hands white-knuckled the steering wheel. She gunned the engine and screeched the tires. It jolted in first gear then second. At the corner of Main Street, she suddenly stopped the car without gearing down. The car lurched and sputtered until she pushed in the clutch. My body flew forward against the shoulder belt. Wind-whipped trees blazed. Black smoke billowed in whirling clouds from a truck on fire. Glenda put the A/C on to recirculate. Hot air blew out of the vents.

"Where should I go?" Glenda's voice shook.

"Turn LEFT!" I yelled. Sweat poured off my body and the car filled with the stink of fear.

"WHERE?" Glenda gunned the gas pedal again. The car lurched forward as she worked the gearshift.

Thick tunnels of black smoke roiled along the street and up into the sky like a disaster movie. Aliens were coming, or the Walking Dead, or it was the Zombie Apocalypse. My brain couldn't decide what was happening. "GO NORTH!" I yelled. "HIGHWAY 12!"

Everybody in Lytton knew that Main Street turned into Highway 12, the Lytton-Lillooet Highway. Why didn't Glenda know that? Wasn't she the adult here? I shook my head and thumped my legs with my fists. None of this was real. None of this was possible. The whole village was on fire.

Glenda's car crawled along Main Street. Everything was on fire. There was a huge bang. A barbecue tank had exploded.

"LOOK!" I yelled. The supermarket was on fire. The café was on fire. The liquor store was on fire. The bank and seniors' home were on fire. The health centre was on fire. People were running. Cars and trucks drove in every direction. People ran for their vehicles. Parked vehicles burned. People driving stopped and picked up people on foot.

"Slow down! I want to get this on video!" Scott yelled.

Mayor Jan Polderman yelled out of his red truck window as he drove past, "GET OUT! NOW! Evacuation order!" Somebody sitting next to him in his truck videotaped the scene.

The stray dog rode in the back of another pickup truck. Glenda turned on the radio. The announcer bellowed: "Mandatory evacuation! Mandatory evacuation for the Village of Lytton and surrounding areas due to extreme danger to persons and property."

"No kidding!" I sneered.

The dash clock showed 6:00 p.m., and the thermostat screamed 49.6 º C. We drove past the Tess's Trees sign. Tess's house and greenhouse were on fire.

Panic ran through me. "STOP! LET ME OUT!"

"WHAT! ARE YOU *CRAZY*?" Glenda yelled. "There's no one there. Their vehicles are gone."

"I don't care! STOP!" I ordered.

Glenda pulled the car onto the shoulder, and it jolted to a stop. The engine chugged again and again, and then stalled.

I hopped out of the car and ran across the street. Massive flames growled and screamed, swallowing the wooden planks of Tess's house. Next to the house, panes of glass on the greenhouse blew out, shattering in the intense heat. The heat of the flames scorched my face. Tire tracks shouted from the dirt driveway that they were gone. "Thank God." I wiped my face with my hands and turned.

"HURRY," Scott yelled through the car window.

My pulse raced. My mind felt like a pile of toppled bricks. "You're right. They left." I imagined Tess running from her house.

I yanked the Tess's Trees sign from the post, ran across the street, narrowly missed being hit by a truck and got back into the car, tossing the sign onto the backseat beside Scott.

"Idiot!" Scott said. This time, he wasn't joking.

"Now where?" Glenda said. "I don't know where I'm going."

"Drive!" I yelled. "Go to Lillooet." This was nothing like gaming or any movie.

WEDNESDAY JUNE 30

on the road from Lytton to Lillooet

It was hard to see the highway. Thick smoke rolled and roiled and suffocated the valley.

"Get out of the way!" Glenda yelled at the truck in front of us. The traffic crawled. People videotaped the fire through their windows, causing a backup. Tail lights flashed and were the guides that kept us on the road.

"We'll be okay," I said, gasping to catch my breath. "Don't panic." I was talking more to myself than to Glenda and Scott. Adrenaline ripped up and down my arms and neck. I sat forward in the seat and leaned over the dash, trying to see better through the smoke.

People honked, urging everyone to speed up.

The line of cars and trucks followed each other like the riveted sections of a centipede. Brake lights flashed off and on. Sirens screamed. Fire trucks whipped past.

"Hurry up!" Glenda yelled again at the drivers ahead. "What's the hold up?"

"Move, people!" I burst out. Suddenly, road rage seemed acceptable. No one drove fast enough.

"There's a fire behind us! Hurry up!" Scott added.

Once we passed the worst of the village smoke, we could see farther. But even still, giant waves of smoke roiled along the road. I kept looking in the rear-view mirror. Terrifying flames engulfed our village. Overwhelmed, my throat burned and tears sprang from my eyes. I couldn't stop the flow. Here I was, being responsible, and I felt like a little kid — helpless.

Once we rounded a bend in the road, the flames were no longer visible. My pulse raced. My breathing came in shallow gusts.

"Scott! What about your folks?" Glenda asked.

"I texted them. They're heading to Lillooet, too," he said, his voice shaky.

"Grab my phone from my purse, Jack," Glenda said. "Phone your mom."

"Mom is going to freak out."

I coughed to clear my throat. It was raw. I fished around inside Glenda's purse between us on the console. Her cell phone was in the front pocket.

"My security code is 9111."

"Sick joke," I said.

"What's so sick about that?" Glenda sounded defensive.

"It's an emergency," I said, unlocking her phone. "It seems ironic, that's all."

"Don't sass me!"

"I'm not!" I liked Glenda, but anger took hold of me. I found "Cindy" in her contacts. After I pressed the call sign, it rang once before I heard my mom's voice in my ear.

"Hi, Glenda. What's happening? What's Jack been up to now?" Mom was all business.

"Mom, it's me," I said. My voice sounded young and afraid.

"What's wrong, Jack?" she gasped.

"We had to leave the house, Mom. It's on fire! There was nothing I could do!" Tears rushed down my face.

"This is no time for jokes, Jack. Put Glenda on."

I hesitated for a moment. It did sound unbelievable. "Mom, the whole village is on FIRE!" My voice shook. "No joke!"

"Oh my gosh. Did you leave the coffee maker on?"

"NO! I DIDN'T!" I burst out crying harder.

"No joke?" Her voice was scary-serious. "I'm so sorry, Jack! I didn't mean it! You know I love you."

"No joke, Mom," I wailed. "Scott and I were in the basement. Glenda got us out." My arms and legs shook uncontrollably. I realized then that we could have died. I tried to brush away my tears, but they kept coming. Snot filled my nose. I snuffled but the snot became liquid and streamed onto my t-shirt.

"Are you okay? Where are you? What are you doing? Have you talked to your father?"

"Slow down ... one question at a time." I couldn't handle her rapid-fire questions. My pulse increased again. "Scott and I are with Glenda. She's driving us to Lillooet. I'm gonna try to find Dad's office."

73

"He's gone north to oversee the forest fire crews. Remember?" Mom said. "Ask Glenda to get a motel room and I'll pay for it with my credit card over the phone. I'm coming."

"Mom, don't come. We'll be fine," I said. "I don't want you making a big deal out of everything."

"Put her on speaker," Glenda said.

I touched the button to release Mom's voice into the car.

"I just turned on the TV. Lytton is on the news! Oh NO, Jack! This IS a HUGE DEAL. Our house just burned down. I'll drive back tomorrow."

"Cindy!" Glenda said. "You just got to Victoria. Rest a day. I can take care of getting a motel room. Drive back the following day."

"Okay. I'll phone Rob and see what's happening. I'll see if he can come."

"No, don't bother him. We'll be fine for a couple of days." Glenda sounded sure of herself now that we were far away from Lytton, far away from the fire.

"Jack, will you be okay?" Mom asked. "Today is Wednesday. I'll drive back on Friday."

"Yeah, I'll be okay." The stench of smoke filled the car. I smelled my hand. It stank like smoke, but the A/C was finally blowing cool air. My pulse was slowing down a bit and I gulped a few breaths.

"Drive safely, Glenda. Phone me later." Mom paused. "I love you, Jack," she said.

Mom never said "I love you." It felt strange. Traffic was heavy and I wanted to scream at all the trucks and cars in front of us to get out of our way.

WEDNESDAY JUNE 30

Lillooet, the day of the wildfire

Vehicles filled the town of Lillooet. It was bigger than Lytton, and I always felt like I was in a city when I was there, but according to the town's sign, the population was only around 7,000. Glenda pulled into the Four Pines Motel and parked. She went into the office while Scott and I stayed in the car and turned the ignition back on to let the A/C blow on us.

"I can't believe what just happened," I said to Scott. My legs and arms still shook.

"Yeah, this is unreal." He tapped on his phone, texting.

When Glenda came out, she looked grim. "They're full."

Glenda drove along until she came to another hotel, the Hotel DeOro. "Jack, go in the office and ask if they have a room."

Inside, the hotel clerk said, "Sorry, young man, the hotel

is full." The lobby was buzzing with activity. People were coming and going, and some were crying as if they'd come from Lytton, too.

Farther down the road, Glenda pulled into Hotel Victoria. It was also full. "Now what?" Glenda said when she got back in the car.

"I'll search online to see if there's anywhere else to stay," Scott offered. "And I have to find my parents." He tapped his phone to message his parents, and Glenda found a gas station to top up.

"No word yet," Scott said.

"You can hang out with us," I said. "Not sure where we'll be staying, but at least we have this car to get around in." I suddenly felt grateful to Glenda.

"Okay, I found another place in town," Scott said. "It's Canada's Best Value Inn. It's on 6th and Main. Go back the way we came, and then turn left on 6th Street."

"Got it." Glenda started her car and found the last hotel in Lillooet.

"It's a no go," Glenda said when she returned from the hotel office. She looked defeated. "But apparently there are cots and food at the Lillooet & District REC Centre for evacuees."

"Let's go," I said. "I'm starved." My stomach was telling me it was time for food. I noticed the dash clock said 9:00 p.m. already. It had taken a long time to get to Lillooet, plus it was taking a long time to find a place to stay.

Scott said, "It's back at the other end of town, where we first came in." He directed Glenda to drive straight down Fraserview Street back onto Main Street.

As we pulled up, we could see a crowd gathered around a barbecue and tables. Grassy lawns surrounded the centre and wooden picnic tables anchored beneath massive weeping willow trees. Glenda parked, and we all joined the food line in the waning twilight. My stomach felt like a hollow cave. People talked loudly, some cried, some were angry. By the time we had plates of food and found a place to sit, the sun had sunk, and lights on the REC Centre glowed across the grass.

"How are you folks doing?" An older man came and stood at the head of our picnic table while we ate hot dogs.

"Okay," I said. All I was thinking about was finishing off my hot dogs. Ketchup and mustard oozed out all over my fingers. Glenda handed me a napkin.

"Good dogs," Scott mumbled with his mouth full.

"I think we're in shock," Glenda said. "I tried to find a hotel room, but every place in town is full." She was on the verge of tears.

The man's pen poised over a form on a clipboard. "What are your names?"

After we told him, he said, "There's room in the centre, but it's cooler outside. You can bunk here until you know your next step."

"Thank you," Glenda said to the man. "We'll stay for the night."

"My dad texted," Scott said. "He said his phone battery was dead before. They're in Merritt at the evacuation centre. He said there's lots of room there."

"Tell him we'll head to Merritt tomorrow." Glenda wiped her eyes and picked at her hot dog.

* * *

Outside at the centre, I tossed and turned on the cot all night. My muscles were tense, and I felt keyed up. I couldn't relax. There were insects buzzing around, and random people talking, smoking, laughing and crying. I must have fallen asleep at some point because morning finally came. I was exhausted and panicked. Like the low point of a game, my life in Lytton was gone. I wondered when my next life would start.

THURSDAY
JULY 1

the day after the wildfire, morning

It was Canada Day, but there was no celebration. A heavy cloud hung over the REC centre yard as people stirred.

"Let's get out of here," I told Glenda when she yawned and sat up. I felt gross. My throat was raw from yelling, crying and the smoke.

Glenda looked rough. Her hair free-floated from the elastic that had corralled it yesterday.

"I need coffee." She got up, stumbling, and found the coffee setup on a table by the recreation centre door.

"Morning!" Scott said.

"Why are you so cheerful?" I asked.

"It's good to be alive," he said. "Thanks for letting me tag along."

It struck me then how Scott might still feel like an outsider. "Hey, any time."

Scott hugged me. It was quick and hard, like he really needed it. It felt good, but we didn't linger. It was too awkward. I needed that hug, though. It kept me from going over the edge to despair.

People worked at cookstoves and a barbecue, making breakfast. Sausages sizzled on the grill, and pancakes and eggs cooked on the industrial griddle.

"Let's get some food before we hit the road," I said. I punched Scott on the arm and smiled at him. He smiled back and it was all okay for that moment. We'd gone through something big together. We were changed and we didn't quite know what to do with the weird new feeling of being glad to be alive.

Glenda carried cups of coffee with lids for all of us to a picnic table. Scott and I brought plates of food for ourselves and one for her.

"I hope we can go home today. Maybe the house wasn't damaged too badly?" I said.

Glenda looked at me with a mix of surprise and sympathy. "In case you've forgotten, flames were eating your house when we left." Her tone was deadpan.

The memory of the flames coming from the bedrooms at the back of the house flashed inside my mind.

"I think the town is a complete write off," Glenda continued. "I've been reading updates on my phone." To prove it, she showed me a news report, a village social media site and then a school group of which she and my mom were both members. "So far, the school survived the fire, but not much else."

It struck me then how defeated everyone looked there

hunched over their breakfasts, but how cheerful all the volunteers were. I thought about Rick Green's assignment and how he'd say something about the portrait of a town. I snapped a photo of the volunteers cooking breakfast.

After we ate, we went and thanked the volunteers for breakfast and then we got into Glenda's car to head to Merritt.

"Before we hit the highway, let's grab another coffee." Glenda drove to the Tim Hortons drive-thru, and she ordered us all dark-roast coffee with shots of espresso.

"I didn't know you could do that," I said. "Extra sugar for me."

My coffee tasted strong but good.

"Your mom texted," Glenda said. "I told her to meet us in Merritt at the evacuation centre."

"Okay," I said. "Did she say anything about my dad and sister?" I asked. I was used to my dad overseeing forest fires, but this year was different. We had our own fire.

"Here. Use my phone while I drive," Glenda said. "It takes about two hours and thirty minutes to get there."

I found the text from my mom, and I got Quinn's and Dad's cell numbers from her.

Hey Dad, where are you? I texted.

Then I texted: *Hey Quinn, how are you?* I held the phone for a long time, until we got to Merritt, but there were no replies. I wasn't worried. It helped that I'd known Glenda since I was a little kid. She felt like family although we'd never left Lytton together. Still, she could be the responsible one now who knew how to get to Merritt, and I could sit with my feelings and ruminate.

"Scott, I need directions," Glenda said.

Scratch that, I thought. *I guess she needs help navigating.*

"I'm on it." Scott tapped on his cell phone. "Do you want the safest route, or the fastest?"

"The safest," Glenda and I both said.

"Okay. Here it is. Merritt Civic Centre, 1950 Mamette Avenue. The route is Cache Creek to Kamloops then on to Merritt."

After what felt like an endless drive, Glenda drove into Merritt. Canadian flags at half-mast lined the main street alongside orange placards saying, "Cancel Canada Day." Kids' shoes of various sizes, styles and colours crowded the steps of the Provincial Building. It was a memorial to the Kamloops residential school children. I thought about Rory and his family. I felt sad for everyone who lost children in residential schools. It really wasn't a day to celebrate. All the sadness from the Lytton fire and the children piled on top of each other like a black cloud. I felt like a mountain lion was stalking me.

The phone in my hand rang.

"Jackhammer!" It was Quinn's voice on the other end.

"Our house burned down," I sobbed. Tears ran down my face. I'd felt better when I woke up, but now it felt like the night before all over again.

"It's okay, bud. It's just stuff. I'm so glad you're okay!" Her voice sounded happy.

It was so good to hear her voice, and it made me glad to know she wasn't upset with me about the house burning down. I didn't know what had caused the fire, but I felt responsible because I was the only family member there at the time. "I'm so sorry . . ." I choked out.

"It's NOT your fault." Her words had force and conviction. *She must be telling the truth*, I thought. She always told the truth.

"Thanks for that." I let her words sit like a cool cloth on my hot heart. "I love you." The words seemed necessary and not awkward, even though I'd never said them to her before.

"I love you too, Jackhammer. Stay strong," she said.

"I will." I gulped a lungful of air and held it. It calmed me.

"Gotta go, but I'll call again soon." She hung up.

I didn't feel strong, but I needed to be. I thought about all the video games I'd played, all the movies I'd watched, all the heroes who'd overcame hard times. They set out on missions, they met danger with bravery and overcame every obstacle. This mission, this problem was the environment changing and biodiversity in danger. And without lots of natural places, the Earth was less able to cope. It was happening and people could make a difference, but I was only fourteen years old. What could I do?

The phone rang in my hand again. This time it was my dad.

"Hey, Son," he said. "Sorry it's taken awhile to get to a place with cell service. I'm in northern B.C."

"Do all the trees die in a forest fire?" I suddenly needed to know.

My dad was quiet for a second. "Mostly, yes. But remember . . . coniferous trees drop cones, and forest fires open the cones. Then their seeds fall into the ground and grow new trees." His voice was breaking up a bit, but I could still hear him. "Except for lodgepole pines. They have thick bark and can withstand fires."

"That's amazing," I said. "Does that mean more of those will be planted?"

"Yes. The guys with white coats are always working on hybrids." He coughed. It must have been smoky there, too.

"But Lytton's fire wasn't a forest fire, Son," Dad said.

"Really?" I said. "How do you know?"

"It was human-caused, I saw on the news. Maybe a train sparked it, or a cigarette butt or a campfire," Dad said. "It could have been anything in that heat. Anyway, it's under investigation. Love you, Son. I'm so glad that you're okay."

"Love you, too, Dad."

"We'll go riding when I see you next, okay?"

"Okay, Dad." I tapped the red off button.

I was relieved knowing that I for sure had not started a house fire and burned down the entire village. That would be too much to live with. I suddenly felt like a mountain lion crouched nearby, waiting to pounce.

THURSDAY JULY 1

Merritt, one day after the wildfire

We checked into the Merritt Civic Centre with a registration clerk sitting sentry at a table.

"I need your information for the Evacuee Registration and Assistance web portal. It's run by the B.C. government," the elderly man said. "You'll qualify for assistance for things like temporary housing and other things which your insurance may not cover."

"Got it," Glenda said. She gave them her ID, but I didn't have any. They had to take my word for who I was. They liked that Glenda was a teacher. She could verify my identity.

The clerk tapped our information into the computer. "You can stay here for a week, if need be," he said.

"Geeze, I hope we don't have to stay here for a week," Glenda said. "No offense. I'm heading back to Ontario to my family."

"When will you leave?" I didn't want to be stranded there myself. My arms and legs tensed, and panic rose in my throat. What if my mom didn't show up? What if I was marooned there with no one?

"Not til after your mom is here. Don't worry, Jack." Glenda put her arm around my shoulders and squeezed.

An attendant directed us to get lunch from the kitchen while it was still available. They had pre-packaged sandwiches, cookies, apples, juice boxes and, after lunch, ice-cream sandwiches.

Scott's parents finally found him at the centre while we were eating. They hugged and cried. Scott said, "Thanks for driving me here, Glenda." He hugged her, too. "See you around, you animal," he said to me. We pumped our knuckles together. I impulsively hugged Scott again, then wrestled with him for a minute or two to show him how much I loved him and appreciated his friendship.

When we were done wrestling, he said, "Let me know if you get a phone plan."

I knew my mom had his number in her cell phone, so we could contact each other again soon.

"For sure." I grinned and waved as he left. I would probably see him later. Wouldn't I? This summer was supposed to be in Lytton, and now panic stalked me, not knowing what the future held. Where would Scott's parents take him? I shook my head to try to settle down.

There was nothing to do, and it was a hot day in Merritt, even if it felt cooler than Lytton had been the past while. The heat wave was brutal. The heat dome was brutal. Maybe there would be a severe heat dome every summer. And with that, there would always be the danger of wildfires. Fear bristled through me. The black cloud filled my head. I felt the hair on my arms and neck stand on end.

"Your mom will be here tomorrow," Glenda said. "I won't leave until she's here."

I felt relieved. My nerves calmed down a bit.

* * *

Glenda and I hung around at the front of the centre, trying to relax on bright plastic lawn chairs. More volunteers came, and truckloads of donations arrived and were unloaded into the centre. People from Lytton streamed to the centre. Then there was Tess. I couldn't believe my eyes when I saw her. The black cloud in my head eased up.

"Hey!" I said, smiling like a dork.

"It's you!" Tess ran over and threw her arms around me. "You're okay!" She hugged me tight, digging her head into my chest. She felt nice there, in my arms.

"Yo, dork," said Kallie, punching me on the arm.

"Peace!" smiled Jaime. She held up two fingers against my face.

I reluctantly pulled away from Tess. At the last moment before she went out of reach, I caught her hand in mine. It was a risk, but I didn't want to let her go. Remembering the sight of her house on fire sent chills through me. "I'm so glad you got away from the fire okay."

Tess squeezed my hand. "This is so crazy. I don't even know what happened. There was so much traffic, and we didn't know where to go. We slept in our truck last night.

And we had the stray dog with us." She pulled her hand out of mine.

I wondered if she was friend-zoning me.

"Man, do you ever stink," Jaime said, punching my arm. "I hope they have showers here." She wrinkled her nose.

"Let's get free stuff," Kallie said. "I don't have anything with me. Just the outfit I'm wearing."

We all lined up and Glenda joined us. The volunteers had organized all the donations into sections inside the centre. I trailed along behind the girls once we began loading up on stuff. There were toiletries, clothes, shoes, toys, books — you name it, and it was all free. There were even bikes in a room at the back.

After I selected a few toiletries and a couple changes of clothes, someone pushed a new backpack into my arms. "Thank you," I said. It was some random stranger, but the look of pity in their eyes felt overwhelming. I heard the word "victim" over and over again. My throat tightened and tears sprang to my eyes. I'd never been a victim before. It made me feel weak and powerless. And I wasn't used to anyone giving me things.

Glenda and the girls went to have showers in the ladies' change room, and I headed off to the men's showers. It felt great to get cleaned up, to wash off the stink and ash from the fire. If I had a complaint, it was only one. I didn't like the shampoo. It smelled weird. It wasn't Quinn's home-made peppermint shampoo. That had all burned up in the fire. After the shower, I dressed in the new orange t-shirt and other clothes, and I stuffed my dirty stuff into my backpack with my other new outfit.

* * *

In the large room, which had an open kitchen on the side, volunteers placed salads, deli meats and fresh buns on the long counter. We all lined up to get food again. I looked at the clock on the wall. It was 6:00 p.m. They were punctual about meals around here, it seemed. Tess smiled and leaned against my shoulder. It felt nice.

The food was okay, but my taste buds were a bit off. Maybe it was from all the smoke in the air? As I ate, my mind returned to thoughts of Lytton and how my home was probably completely gone. I couldn't believe it. I had to see it myself. I bet Mom would want to see our house, too. I had to get her to drive us back there and see.

FRIDAY JULY 2

Merritt, two days after the wildfire

While I waited for my mom to arrive, Tess and her friends said, "See you later!" They found bikes and went for a ride down the road. I wondered where they were going. *Maybe I could use one of the bikes, too?*

"Do you mind if I go for a ride?" I said to Glenda. Merritt had light forest fire smoke, probably from far away, and it wasn't too hot.

Glenda followed my gaze to the girls riding down the street. "Tagging along with the girls?" She smiled.

"No. They didn't ask."

Her face softened. "Be back by dinnertime." I left my backpack with Glenda and went in search of a bike. I found an old mountain bike at the back end of the civic centre. It would have to do. I didn't want to sit around all afternoon waiting for my mom and the girls. I had to get my legs moving, and biking would help to work out the anxiety about the fire.

"Whereabouts are there bike trails?" I asked the old man inside the civic centre. Like Lytton, I figured Merritt had to have trails. Lots of people liked to bike in the area.

"Head over to Voght Street," he said, pointing. "Follow it until you get to Grimmet Street, which will take you to Allen Road. Then you'll see the hill ahead to the Tom Lacey Trail. It's all uphill, but there's a great view."

"Wow," I said, surprised. "Sounds perfect."

"I ride there whenever I can," the man said. "Here, you'll need this." He handed me a bottle of water from the cases under the table.

I looked at him more closely. He was old, but also trim and muscular. "The trail sounds amazing," I said.

"Have fun." He smiled. "That old bike took me on many good rides."

"Thanks for letting me use it. I used to ride a lot. My dad works in forestry. He said the heat dome made it too dangerous to ride in the forest."

The man scowled. "Darn heat." He handed a clipboard to a group of people beside me. They were from Lytton, too. "Stay hydrated," he said to me. "And it should be fine if you stay on the trail. That part of the forest doesn't have much tinder." He turned away to talk to the new registrants.

* * *

The afternoon felt like a perfect summer day. Except for the ever-present forest-fire smoke and the dark cloud that hung over me. I was tired of it, but there wasn't anything I could do about it. Anxiousness riddled my muscles. I drove my legs hard against the pedals.

I found the trail without any trouble. A sign said Tom Lacey Memorial Trail, and a hard-packed path ran off into the trees. The donated clothing felt new and stiff on me, which made riding uncomfortable at first.

The breeze felt good. My heart pounded and pounded, but I didn't let up. Flames and the roiling black smoke flashed in front of my eyes. My legs tingled as they released the feelings of fear and horror. I shook my head to clear my vision.

When I got to a viewpoint, I stopped to drink. The smoke made it hard to see far, but what I could see didn't look good. The forests and river valleys snaked off into the distance. I could see where massive plumes of smoke funnelled into the sky. I felt horribly alone with no home, no village, no familiarity, adrift in a sea of mountainous nothing — hopeless. My stomach rolled.

It didn't help to look out and see evidence of logging around me. While the climate was always changing, people were driven by greed instead of concern about how to best manage our forest. I snapped a photo portrait of the area, facing west from Merritt toward Lytton. I imagined the future with more conservation areas. The forest would regenerate, wouldn't it?

Though adrenaline and endorphins coursed through me, I felt that black cloud of fear ride my back like a mountain lion on its prey. I jumped up and down to shake it off, but when I stopped, it gripped me again. At one point, I noticed I was shaking, and I couldn't stop.

A man and woman biked over and stopped to drink water at the viewpoint next to me. "Nice day for a ride," the woman said.

"This summer has been a rough one, though," the guy added.

"Tell me about it," I said. I didn't want to tell them about escaping Lytton, so I stood quietly looking at the view. I hoped they didn't notice my tremors. Life felt cruel and unfair.

"I've never seen a heat dome like this the two decades we've been here," the guy said. "And this isn't going away."

"That sucks," I said.

"It will continue to dry out more and more in this area," he went on. "Our way of life will change. Imagine. Here we are in thirty-degree heat, and it feels like it's cooling off. We'll have floods and mudslides next."

"Really?" I said. "How do you know?" I was already incredibly gloomy and this guy was adding to it. I wished he hadn't ridden up the hill today. I wished I'd never met him or had to listen to his doomsday predictions.

"That's what happens when you strip the land." He turned to the woman he was with. "We'd better head out," he said, returning his water bottle to its holder on his bike frame.

I wasn't sure what he meant. Did he mean that the fires stripped the land, or was it logging? Maybe it was both. Before I could ask him what he'd meant, he rode away down the trail.

"See you around," the woman said as she pedaled after him.

I hoped not. I felt grumpy and agitated while the day wore

on. I didn't want to see those people again, and since I didn't know the trails, I decided to ride back the way I'd come.

* * *

When I got back to town, I saw Tess. The stray dog was with her.

"Hey," she said as I returned to the centre. "Want to come swimming with us?" She had on a swimsuit and a pair of shorts over top, and she had the dog on a leash.

I sympathetically petted the dog's head. "Good boy," I said.

"We're going to the Nicola Valley Aquatic Centre." Kallie and Jaime fidgeted with odd items from their swim bags.

"Sure," I said. I tried to sound cool, even though I felt excited about hanging out with Tess. I looked down at my shorts. They'd have to pass for swimming trunks.

"Hey, boy." I petted the dog some more. He panted while he walked at the end of his new leash with Tess. I was happy to see he'd found a good person to take care of him.

"I have to leave the dog with my parents."

We went with Tess to Intown Inn & Suites as she held the dog's leash, then we waited outside under the hotel's office awning while she took the dog inside.

As we walked to the pool, she said, "Ninety per cent of Lytton is gone. I'm glad I found this dog. He got away from us when we evacuated, and we had to go find him on a logging road."

"Yeah, you should have seen us! Tess even threw biscuits to a bear to get him to stop following us!" Jaime said.

"Crazy. Glad you got him." Horrible images of the village on fire filled my head again. I blinked my eyes quickly a few times to dislodge the images and tried to focus on going swimming. The pool wouldn't be like our swimming hole back in Lytton, but it was something. It also wouldn't be like our Lytton pool, which was outside. It was inside a building, but it was all we had that day. It would have to be enough.

"There's a bus tour of Lytton the day after tomorrow. I want to see if my house survived," Tess said. She pushed her hair away from her eyes. "You going?"

"Maybe." I had no idea what my mom planned. "We might drive there by ourselves."

"You can't," Tess said. "No personal vehicles allowed."

"Then I guess we're going. I want to see if there's anything left of my house, too."

Walking to the pool, I held Tess's hand gently again for a few minutes and when she pulled her hand away, she held onto my arm as we walked through the centre. I didn't tell her that it felt like a mountain lion was near.

FRIDAY JULY 2

two days after the wildfire, evening

My mom arrived at the Merritt Civic Centre just before they shut down supper. She clung onto me and pretty much wouldn't let go until I pulled her hands apart from behind my neck.

"I could have lost you," she sobbed. "I watched the news over and over before I left. It's all I thought about all day." Mom rubbed her eyes with a tissue.

"Yeah, but you didn't lose me. Just everything else." I wanted her to get a grip on herself. Maybe if I changed the topic, she might ease up. "You'd better get some food before they put it all away."

After supper, we took turns talking on her cell phone with Dad and Quinn.

"I talked about this with your mom," Dad began when it was my turn on the phone. "We decided to get you a cell phone plan so you can phone us on your own. Consider it a graduation present, from middle school." He sounded pleased.

It would be good to have service on the phone I carried around in my pocket. "That's great." I'd be able to keep in touch with Rory, Scott and Tess.

"I'll meet up with you and your mom once the fires die down here."

"When will that be? The end of summer?" My shoulders slumped. Just when we needed him most because of the fire, he couldn't come.

"When I can," he said. "I love you, Son. Stay strong for your mother." He hung up.

I shook myself then. *He's right*, I thought. *I must decide to be strong. I've got this.* My body might not agree, but I had to try to be strong for Mom.

* * *

After supper, Mom and Glenda settled into the bright chairs at the front of the centre to visit. Glenda told Mom about her plan to leave in the morning to drive to Ontario.

"I want to go to Lytton tomorrow to see if our house is still standing," Mom said.

"You have to sign up for the bus tour at the registration desk," Glenda said. "I'm sure my place is gone. I'll deal with insurance from my parents' home."

Mom looked super annoyed. "I hate being in limbo."

"What about the phone plan for me? Can we do that now?"

"Yeah, let's." Mom got to work talking to her cell phone plan provider. She added me to her plan, but I had to help pay my bill once I was working.

"You'll have to wait until we get to Victoria for your SIM card. They'll mail it there. But here's your new number." Mom wrote it down on a small notepad from her purse.

I remembered something else. "I left something in your car, Glenda."

SATURDAY JULY 3

three days after the wildfire

"Mind if I take off for a while?" I said after breakfast. "Tess invited me to go to Rotary Park." There was a spray park there. "We'll be far away from any fires," I assured Mom.

A TV in the corner played the news. Images of forest fires from around the province filled the screen. Mom was transfixed. "Don't be long."

I didn't pay much attention to her comment since I knew I had nothing to do until the bus tour. She might have had insurance to deal with over the phone, but she didn't need me around for that.

Tess, Kallie, Jaime and the dog came to meet me outside the evacuation centre. I hid something for Tess behind my back. She smiled when she saw me.

"This is for you," I said, pulling her hand-painted Tess's Trees sign from behind my back.

"What? How'd you get that?" She grabbed the sign from me and hugged it. Tears sprang to her eyes.

My throat was too rough and dry to speak. All I could do was hug her awkwardly with the sign between us.

* * *

After we dropped the sign off with Tess's parents at their hotel, we walked to Rotary Park. Tess held the dog's leash.

I said to Tess, "What are you going to name him?"

"Sparky. Because he came out of the fire." She looked proud as she walked with the dog by her side, and Sparky looked happy, too. Happier than when he hung out with me. I guess Tess took better care of him.

"He's happy with you."

Tess smiled. "He's a good dog." She patted his side as we walked.

* * *

The walk to the park took a while. I remembered how I'd first met Tess during the club fair at school. Then I'd seen her at the village market giving out pamphlets. She really cared about the environment, and she knew what to do. I suddenly knew what I wanted to do, too.

"I'm joining your club."

Tess smiled. "Really? Give me your phone."

I laughed and handed it over. She tapped a number into it. "It's my mom's cell number for now, but when I get my own phone, I'll let you know my number."

A warm feeling spread across my chest. I knew we were solid friends now and she wanted to keep in touch wherever we went from here.

* * *

At Rotary Park, we saw Scott and his parents at the tables near the waterpark. Scott joined us as we ran in and out of the spray with Sparky. The dog loved the cool water, and we all laughed watching him. I even forgot about the fire for a little while. But once we stopped, it felt like a mountain lion was stalking me again.

We stretched out on the grass and rested with Sparky. The massive willows waved above us while Kallie and Jaime teased each other and Scott.

"What do you want me to do for the club?" I asked Tess.

"You could help with web stuff," Tess said. "A new website, social media."

"Sure," I said. I was grateful to Mr. Marconi then for getting me to write lots this past semester in English, otherwise I wouldn't have wanted to create a website.

Scott sat up and leaned against the tree. "Tell me more."

Tess began as she sat up, too. "Did you know that it's really important to have natural places? Places where trees, plants, waterways, animals and birds are left to their own natural ecosystems?"

"Yeah, sure," Scott agreed. "Who'd argue with that?"

"When people disturb the land and systems, it isn't as resilient." She turned to face us on the grass. "A biodiverse system has all it needs to sustain itself, and people can manage those systems rather than simply aiming for profit. Land that is overused will become sterile in time. A good example of a healthy, people-run, biodiverse ecosystem is a small mixed farm, or a yard with gardens."

"So this club teaches about that?" Scott asked.

"If we don't teach kids how important it is, parts of the world could be devastated with erosion, floods and fires."

"Hey, let's do a group photo for the new site," I said.

Tess, Kallie, Jamie and Scott gathered around me.

Scott sat at the back since he was tallest. "I want in to the club, too," he said.

Jaime poked him with her elbow. "I guess we can let you in." She laughed.

As I held up the phone to snap a photo, Sparky got into the frame, too. We all sat with our backs to the massive weeping willows, and we made faces and peace signs. I snapped a second photo, one that didn't have any goofiness. Rick Green would like these. I thought of what I'd write about us. *Biodiversity rules.* That's what I'd say.

"Anyone can join, anywhere."

It was strange joining a school club during summer holidays.

MONDAY
JULY 5

five days after the wildfire

The first leg of the bus trip would take two and a half hours. Scott and his family were on the bus, as was Tess and her family, and Rory would meet us with Colleen at Lillooet.

"Hey!" Rory yelled when he saw me. He piled on top of me, then we found seats together. Colleen sat with my mom. Lillooet to Lytton would take almost an hour.

"We're camping near Boston Bar, at the Tuckkwiowhum Village," Rory said. "It's cool there. There's a campsite, teepees and everything. Their longhouse has a ton of donations, so we're volunteers there."

"Are you staying there long?" I asked. It was cool how the First Nations community came together to support everyone.

"Probably til all the donations are gone. Then we'll head back to Kamloops."

I felt a pang, missing my best friend, but I knew it was selfish. They were doing important work.

When our bus got close to Lytton, we passed Tess's place, where the Tess's Trees sign used to be. I remembered her face when I gave her the sign. But her place was all burned up. There was nothing left of it except for the metal frame of the old greenhouse and the charred post where her sign used to be. I heard Tess cry out from the front of the bus, and my throat went tight. I fought back tears and Rory bumped my side as a signal of support.

The bus took us through the village from the north end to the south end of Main Street. The Hans Knakst Tsitxw (Helping Hands) Society Reaching Out Centre was gone. The Lyl' Towne Deli & Sandwich Shop was gone. The Klowa Art & Café was gone. The Super Foods was gone. The Chinese History Museum was gone. Almost everything along Main Street was gone. The bus turned right down First Street to Fraser Street. As we drove north along Fraser, I counted all the burned-out houses, their foundations bare and full of rubble, until we got to where our house should have been.

"It's gone. Completely gone," Mom sobbed. I wasn't next to her to put my arm around her shoulders and pull her tight against my chest, but I was sure Colleen would comfort her. Then I saw my mountain bike's charred frame. The tires were completely gone, and it was the colour of charcoal. I thought of the bike I'd used in Merritt. I was thankful for it, but it wasn't the same. It wasn't my bike. It didn't fit me right, and I didn't have my helmet. The bus kept moving, and I lost sight of what was left of our home.

Would we ever be able to return? Would my parents rebuild? Everything was a question. Even the village pool was gone.

No place to live, no place to buy food, no place to work. Now what?

"At least the school is still there," Mom said through her sniffling.

"I can't see my place," Rory said. "But the trees looked burned there." He stared across the highway to his old neighbourhood where no houses remained. The electrical lines were all burned up. The village was almost a complete write off, just like Glenda said before. A few random buildings stood in what looked like a scorched war zone.

The trip back to Merritt felt like the longest trip of my life. The bus was completely silent except for sniffling and crying. The fact that I had no house to return to sunk in. I couldn't remember living anywhere else. That house was the only home I'd ever known. My chest felt tight, and my breath came in short bursts.

* * *

The bus stopped at Lillooet where some people had to get off. Rory and Colleen were among them.

"See ya, bud," Rory said, punching me softly when he passed by me to squeeze into the bus's narrow aisle.

I got up so I could give him a real hug. We blocked the aisle and held up others from getting off the bus, but I didn't care. We were two dudes hugging it out. It made me feel happy.

"Going to Victoria?" he said when I finally let him go.

"Probably." I wiped my nose with the back of my hand. I hadn't given it any thought, but it sounded likely, though Mom hadn't said anything about it yet.

"When you come back, let's hang out," Rory said. Then he jogged down the centre aisle, and he was gone.

WEDNESDAY JULY 7

seven days after the wildfire

We planned to leave for Victoria the next morning. I didn't have any choice but to go with my mom to stay with my aunt and my annoying cousins. Besides, I had no summer job to look forward to.

The fire was all over the news still. The CN Rail stopped trains from going through Lytton for three days after the fire. The investigators said they couldn't find evidence that a train started the fire, but all trains had to slow down through B.C. when it was hot and dry.

I was happy to be leaving the evacuation centre. I was having nightmares about the Lytton fire every night. When I had a nightmare, I woke up and lay awake most of the night.

Mom said it might be PTSD, post-traumatic stress disorder. She said I had to start going to counselling right away. She had someone lined up in Victoria, someone my aunt recommended. I hoped counselling would help. I wanted to get better so I could sleep, so I wouldn't feel exhausted all the time.

* * *

I met Scott, Tess, Kallie and Jaime at the pool in Merritt on my last day there. We had a swimming competition, then Jaime timed us again to see who could hold their breath the longest. Kallie won this time. My lungs weren't getting the workouts they were used to anymore.

When we were finished swimming, I went to the men's change room while the girls went to the women's change room. I pulled on my second new outfit, including a blue t-shirt. We all met at the front of the building after we were ready.

"I'm going to miss this pool," Tess said.

"Yeah, it was fun," Scott said. "But not even close to our old swimming hole."

"True," Tess said.

Scott made a peace sign with his fingers. "Peace!" He turned and walked away. He'd picked it up from Jaime.

"We have to keep in touch, Jack. You're doing the website and social media," Jaime reminded me. "We'll have to talk often on the phone. Okay?"

"I remember," I said. How could I forget? If helping would make a difference, I was all in. The girls headed back to the Intown Inn & Suites, and I walked the three blocks with them. It felt good to have a plan even though none of us knew where we would be living in the fall.

"We're going to Florida to stay with my grandparents for a while," Tess said. She pushed her hair behind her ear.

"We leave for Victoria in the morning." Dread crept over me like the prowl of a mountain lion. "It'll be horrible staying with my cousins."

"Bye, dweeb," Kallie said, and disappeared into the hotel.

"At least you're not going to Saskatchewan," moaned Jaime. "It's flatter than a corn tortilla." She gave me a quick hug. "See you soon, turkey." She made a peace sign and left us.

"You're so lucky. I love the ocean." Tess pulled on my hand. "It's beautiful there. I've only been once, when I was a little kid."

I took a firm hold of her hand and pulled her under the awning. I put my arm around her shoulders and buried my face in her damp hair. She smelled like pool chlorine.

"I guess I like walking along the shore and finding gooey ducks. I stomp on the sand next to them and they squirt water. The crabs are cool, too," I said. I pulled Tess around, so she was in front of me.

"I better go," she said, and she stepped away and ran into the hotel.

Clouds gathered in the sky and there was an evening rain shower. It should have felt refreshing, but it didn't. Scott was gone. Rory was gone. Now Jaime, Kallie and Tess were all gone. It felt like a mountain lion was ready to pounce.

MONDAY JULY 19

nineteen days after the wildfire

My aunt said it was the first hot day in Victoria. She had a pool, and my mom enjoyed playing with my cousins in the water.

Counselling was going okay with Stephanie. I was sleeping better, but I still had bad dreams sometimes. Stephanie said I didn't have PTSD but going through a fire had been a traumatic experience. It would take some time to get over, but a full recovery was possible.

My aunt and uncle used to like using their fire table on the patio, but it was off limits for now. The sight of flames freaked me out.

While everyone else had fun in the pool, I worked on my assignment. Mom told me to make a list of all the stuff I lost in the wildfire for insurance, so it could be replaced. When I told Stephanie that I was going to work on the list, she said it would be good to expand on it for counselling purposes.

I remembered learning about tangible and intangible things in English class with Mr. Marconi. He'd said that tangible things were experienced with our senses, and usually, we can put a dollar value on them. But we can't put a value on intangible things.

You'd think it would be exciting to get all new stuff, like it's Christmas. It isn't at all like Christmas. It's exhausting. This was the list I wrote for insurance, and the explanations were for Stephanie.

Bike.

It was the best one I'd ever had. I got it for my birthday last summer. It was only two years old. Some rich kid had it before me and sold it because he crashed it in Kamloops. My dad helped me to get replacement parts. It needed a new front tire, fender, brake calipers and new handlebars. All in all, my dad said it was a great deal because the frame was in perfect shape. To earn the parts, I took care of the chores around the house, like taking out the garbage and cutting the grass. The grass didn't grow much this summer because it was too hot and dry. Bonus.

An image of my burned bike frame came to mind. I blinked rapidly and the image went away.

I decided to leave the bike I'd used in Merritt at the civic centre for someone else since it was too small for me.

Guitar.

It was a gift two Christmases ago. It was left handed, so it was hard to find. Mom ordered it from a store in Vancouver. I quit going to lessons last March. I didn't want to bother learning more songs because I know how to play lots of songs, but I don't plan to play music professionally, so why bother. Mom said I should list it, because it was worth something, and I might like to play more in the future. She has a point. We never know what will happen in the future. I know that more than ever now.

Skateboard.

It was old. I will get to choose a new one. Maybe you think this will be exciting for me, but it won't. I'd rather have my old one back. It was worn just right. The sandpaper top was scuffed right where I put my feet all the time when I rode along Fraser Street and Main Street to Super Foods to buy junk food.

Xbox One game system and five games.

This is what me and my buddies did for fun besides mountain biking. Panic rose in my throat when I thought about June 30th, when Scott and I played video games in the basement before Glenda ordered us from the burning house. I forced a swallow. I crossed the Xbox off my list.

Clothes, books and other random things.

Since we evacuated, Mom bought me all new clothes. As long as I'm comfortable, I'm happy. My mom figured out the cost of the rest of my stuff. I'm glad all my little kid books and toys are gone. I don't need them anyway. Mom says we need to at least replace their cost, then we can donate the money to charity for kids who don't have toys and books. Thinking about giving to other people in need feels good in contrast to how I felt at the evacuation centre when I was pitied. I hated that feeling. I wasn't a victim. I was a survivor.

One house.

My mom is happy about getting to rebuild our house. At least she seems to be trying really hard to put a positive spin on it. Besides getting an entirely new house, we'll have to replace all the furniture, appliances and cabinets. My mom got flyers from a kitchen design store, which shows all kinds of cupboards. I didn't know there were so many kinds of cupboards. Some of the woods are grown in British Columbia, like spruce, pine and poplar. Other kinds of woods are imported. Even though my mom is excited to rebuild the house, Quinn said the town is cursed because Lytton was built on *Kumsheen,* a previous Indigenous peoples' village. She's superstitious. She doesn't think we should rebuild there.

Rory phoned one day and said the Indigenous people in the area said that there is something very special about *Kumsheen*. It is where the Fraser and the Thompson Rivers meet. It has special powers, and they experience special things there. It's private to their culture, so Rory didn't say more. I respect that. Maybe the new town should be called *Kumsheen*, not Lytton.

My home.

Yeah, I already said I lost my house, but home is different than a house. When I say we lost our home, I'm not talking about cupboards. I'm talking about the intangible things like when Quinn still lived with us, and we cooked supper together in the kitchen on the weekend. That was before all the arguing started about Quinn getting a job as a tree planter. Usually, we made pizza.

My mom would buy pizza crust ready to go from Super Foods and we would pick out toppings. My dad liked all the meat he could get. He made meat lover's pizzas. My mom liked veggie pizzas with a bit of ham on them. Quinn liked veggie pizza too, but she also had weird stuff on hers, like artichokes that came in a small can, and sun-dried tomatoes from a bottle. I always had pepperoni pizza, or Hawaiian with ham and pineapple.

Now, when I look at the definition of intangible, I realize that making pizza involves the senses. I can smell pizza baking while I write this, even though there's nothing cooking in the stark white kitchen in my aunt's house in Victoria. I guess the intangible part would be the feeling I had inside that made me feel happy when we were all together. I can't name it, it just was. It isn't anymore, so I lost it. Maybe when we rebuild our house, we can make a new home of it. I hope Quinn comes back. Maybe we will build it somewhere else. Not on *Kumsheen*.

Sense of well-being.

My counsellor helped me to name this thing. I described it as a feeling that my past was all good and happy, and that I used to believe that my future would continue to be the same with lots of happy times with my friends and family. Birthdays, Christmases, holidays. My mom and dad would make special foods and we did something together, like ride the trails. I never used to think about the future. It was like those special times were trail markers, like when we'd go on a ride and there were trees with marks or signs on them, which kept us going on the right path. I'd usually forget about the destination. Instead, I was focused on finding the next marker.

Now I feel like the future is a big black empty place where a mountain lion lives. We don't have markers anymore. My birthday is coming up in August, but I have zero friends in Victoria. My mom has no idea when we will be able to start building our new house, so we are in limbo in Victoria indefinitely.

Motivation for English.

I had the best English teacher ever last year. Everything is going to be online this year, but Mr. Marconi said he wasn't coming back to teach at the school. That is a huge loss for me. Now I don't know if I'll get through high school English. Mom says she can help me with my writing, but I've lost the will for it.

"Why did he have to leave?" I'd asked my mom.

"It was his choice," she'd said. "Since the fire and with the pandemic going on for so long, he's tired of teaching online.

"Well, I liked him." No other teacher had ever let me sit in their chair.

Worst of all, I hadn't seen or spoken to Tess since Merritt. I'd be lying if I said I hadn't thought about her every single day.

WEDNESDAY
AUGUST 24,

almost four months after the wildfire

Before today I was feeling like I didn't really have any friends. None of us were texting each other as much as I thought we would. Maybe I had imagined the feelings I'd had for Tess. She didn't seem interested in me anymore. I decided to try to put her out of my mind and distract myself by watching the Blue Jays.

When I watch baseball, I know Mr. Marconi is watching, too. Then I remember his teacher chair and how good it felt to get to use it for the day. I can't lie — it was nice to get good grades in English. The Jays won their game against the White Sox last night, 2–1.

But today is my birthday and all my friends phoned. Everyone has cell phones with data now. After going through a major fire, all our parents are freaked out, so they want to be able to keep in touch with us. Even Rory's mom let him get a phone, even though Rory wasn't technically in Lytton when the fire happened. Rory and Scott are staying in temporary housing close to Lytton, but too far away from each other to hang out all the time. They said it sucks big time.

"Don't forget you promised to help with the biodiversity club," Tess said on our call. She'd already set up a website, so she gave me the login information. "Sorry I couldn't call from Florida. Mom said we couldn't afford the international rates."

Okay, that explained her lack of contact for most of the summer. I drew in a slow breath.

"You said you'd write all the content," she continued. "Remember? I'm excited you're getting involved."

Remember. How could I not remember my promise to her? "Meh," I said, like it was no big deal.

"Thanks!" Her voice sounded like sunshine. "And happy birthday!"

"Yeah, no problem," I said.

It wasn't like a school assignment. It would be fun. It was the least I could do to help. I wanted to know what was planned for the conservation of wild places. I wanted there to be lots of natural forests in the future for mountain biking and for the good of the planet. A biodiverse landscape could best deal with climate pressures, the pamphlet had said. Most of all, I wanted to spend time with Tess.

"Even though I'm in Whitehorse now, we can work on this together," Tess said. Her mom had a job teaching there for the year, and her dad was an unemployed forestry worker. "We can make it a national club." Her excitement felt contagious.

I was hyped about it, too. "Maybe other kids will want to get involved. We could spread the word to other schools."

"Yeah, like my school in Whitehorse. I plan to get the club going here, then we're going to move back to Lytton later, after the village rebuilds."

"That would be great." I imagined us hanging out by the river. "I miss you."

"Same." She sounded embarrassed. I pictured her blushing. I was glad she couldn't see my face. It felt good to know she missed me too.

After I said goodbye, Quinn said, "I'm proud of you, Jackhammer." She ruffled my hair. "I hope it works out for you."

I grinned.

Quinn took a break from work to come spend time with us after the fire. Then she decided to go to college in the fall. She just found out she was accepted into the Pacific Design Academy, so Mom has been like a box of Pop Rocks all day. "We can help you start your own brand," she said. "And then you can branch out into soaps and shampoos, cosmetics, you name it." Mom was more excited than Quinn.

I'm happy Quinn will be living with us in Victoria. Even Dad flies from Kelowna to spend time with us. His new schedule is two weeks on and two weeks off.

Mom said after we pick up Dad from the airport today, we can stop at the store to get pizza crusts and toppings. We're going to build our own pizzas. The cousins are excited since they've never done this before. Dad said tomorrow he will take me to the Snakes and Ladders biking trails in Saanich. I'm going to kick his butt on the trails with my new bike.

TUESDAY FEBRUARY 7

seven months after the wildfire

Mom and Dad pored over house plans for weeks. They also spent a lot of time talking to friends who had suffered damage from the floods and mudslides in B.C. An eerie feeling crept over me thinking about that guy on the trail in Merritt during evacuation. He'd said that when the forest is stripped, floods and mudslides would come next. Didn't anyone else know that? People had to do things differently. Maybe we couldn't prevent wildfires, but many fires and disasters happened as a result of people misusing the land.

"We can build any style we like, but it has to be the same square footage," Dad said.

Mom tapped on her laptop. "I'll have to do a new search for smaller homes."

It turned out that their insurance wasn't as good as they'd thought, so they had to keep things simple.

We had a boring Christmas and Canadian New Year with the cousins, but Lunar New Year was amazing. Tess had asked for only one thing for Christmas: a flight to Victoria. She said she loved the ocean, and this was her chance to see it again. I was stunned. Did she just want to see the ocean and I was a convenient excuse?

While Mom and Dad, my aunt and Quinn prepared all kinds of special foods, I paced around the house and changed my clothes four times. I finally settled on a plaid shirt and cargo pants. When it was finally time to go to the airport, I made everyone late because I couldn't find my shoes.

Everyone welcomed Tess like she was a long lost relative. Even my mom hugged her and quizzed her for a solid hour about Whitehorse. Quinn gave her a set of her natural soaps.

The next morning, Tess and I went for a walk along the ocean at Spiral Beach. The wind whipped our hair across our faces, but when we ducked behind driftwood and sat with my arm around her to keep her warm, the world could disappear, and I wouldn't care.

"Missed you," I told her.

"Not as much as I missed you," she said, curling into the crook of my arm. "This is chilly, but nothing like Whitehorse. It's minus twenty on a warm day and there's hardly any daylight in the winter." She shivered. "I can't wait to move back south."

After dinner, we all went out into a field to light Chinese lanterns. My aunt said it was okay because it drizzled all day. Now it was cool and clear. The lanterns looked like torches chasing away the mountain lion that stalked me.

To make myself feel better after Tess left, I called Rory.

"There's going to be a planned burn in the forest near Lytton around the beginning of April," he said.

Shivers ran up and down my back. There was the mountain lion again. Talk of fire brought the memory of its smell to my nose. I sniffed a few times. Was something burning?

"Indigenous people used to manage the land that way, and now they need to do it again to make sure a fire won't devastate Lytton again."

"That makes sense." I shuffled around on my chair.

"Plus, archaeologists will supervise the village rubble clearing. There are bound to be special items uncovered."

"Like what?" My curiosity perked up. I liked looking at historic items in museums. Kumsheen was a special place after all, the meeting of two rivers.

"Tools, ceremonial items, who knows? Could be anything." Rory sounded excited.

I relaxed a little. "That's really cool. I hope they find lots of things."

SATURDAY MAY 7

ten months after the wildfire

When I got up today, I chose a green t-shirt to wear with my jeans. It reminded me of one I had back in Lytton. My aunt and cousins dropped us off at the Victoria airport and waved like crazy and called goodbye a million times while I got my bike out of the back of their SUV. Mom and I were flying to Kamloops to meet Dad. I'd insisted on bringing my bike, so once we'd landed, we had an extra-long wait for it at the cargo bay.

"It'd better be worth it," Mom complained.

"A hundred per cent." I grinned, pushing it outside, out to Dad's white forestry truck in the short-term parking.

"Today we move in to our temporary housing." Dad squeezed Mom in a tight hug.

"It's overwhelming." Mom brushed her hair off her face as we got into the truck. She got into the passenger seat next to Dad, and I hopped in the backseat of the crew cab. "I haven't slept in a month," Mom said while she rolled down the window. With Quinn staying at college, it would be just the three of us.

Before we hit the highway to start the long drive to Lytton, Dad went to a Tims drive thru and bought us extra-large coffees and Timbits.

"I'll have a shot of espresso in mine," I said.

The coffee made me more pumped than ever. I couldn't wait to get to Lytton and see my friends. Planning this meet up for weeks had helped to get rid of the black cloud. At times I'd stop and realize that now I felt different. There was no longer a mountain lion stalking me. I felt free. Time had helped. And counselling. But writing about the fire helped me the most because, for me, it came more easily than talking.

After an hour and a half of bland country music, we drove through Lytton and I saw Tess's burned out home again.

"Tess said they're new house will be entirely concrete except for the roof. The roof is going to be steel."

Dad turned down the radio. "The new building codes are going to cost us more. We'll have to trim our plans more. No fancy appliances, Cindy."

The wind whipped Mom's hair around. She rolled up the window and corralled her hair in a pony-tail holder. "I'll sleep better, Jim. It'll be worth it."

Dad picked up Mom's hand and kissed it. "You're worth it."

"Ugh. Get a room you two," I mock-grumbled. Warmth spread across my chest watching my parents. Maybe it was that intangible sense of well-being creeping back.

We couldn't stay in Lytton, but we drove through to get to Boston Bar. All the friends who were rebuilding agreed to meet there. We knew Jaime wasn't coming, or Scott. Scott was already busy working a part-time job. Their families had decided to not return, to collect their insurance money from their burned-out homes. All they had left to do was sell their land as building lots once they were cleared.

We drove down Main Street and saw all the places where we used to go: the Super Foods and the Chinese History Museum, the pool. A pang of excitement welled up inside me. The village would rebuild, and we could move back, maybe even by late fall. It would depend on how long the archaeological work took.

A while later at Boston Bar, Dad parked at our temporary housing. I checked my phone. It was almost time to meet. I unloaded my bike from the back of the truck and took a bottle of water from the cab.

I rode to the trailhead. They were there. Rory, Tess and Kallie.

I hopped off my bike and hugged them all in turn. The fire had changed us all, especially me. I used to be afraid to show affection. Now I was hungry for it and didn't care what others might think.

Tess hung her arms around my neck and pulled my face to her. She kissed me on the cheek.

Rory, who hadn't seen me and Tess together, snickered. "You dog!" He punched me on the arm. Rory and Kallie turned away and kicked at the rocks on the ground. Then we got on our bikes and rode for the hill.

"We're staying in Boston Bar permanently," Rory said. "My mom got a job here, but I'll go to the same school. And we'll hang out lots."

I had a sinking feeling inside. At least I'd still see him regularly after my family moved back to Lytton. "Cool," I said, pedaling hard. Rory kept up, but when I saw that I was getting way ahead of Tess and Kallie, I slowed down and let them catch up.

We rode up the trail through the spring forest. It had been rainy so there were signs of new life everywhere.

At the top of the hill, we stopped to drink water and look over the Fraser Valley. I saw the tail end of a mountain lion slink away through the trees. A shiver ran through me, but I was glad to see there was wildlife here.

From the viewpoint we could see toward Lytton and the burned forests. There was a faint haze of new green shoots. Soon, the forest would grow back in all the burned places.

I took Tess's hand and pulled her under my arm. Kallie and Rory huddled next to us, and we took a group pic for photography class. I thought then that my life wouldn't only be about the loss I went through with the Lytton wildfire, but it would also be about what I'd gained. I knew what I'd write about the moment frozen in the photo. We are survivors.

AUTHOR'S NOTE

Living through a disaster is frightening and difficult. I felt a desire to write about the Lytton fire based on my own experience being impacted by a wildfire. My family and I were just a few of the 80,000 people evacuated from northeastern Alberta during the House River Wildfire in 2016. We left without much notice, and we had no idea what was happening once we'd left.

I thought we'd be away for a few days, but days turned into weeks, and weeks turned into months before I returned home. My family was lucky. Our home was not destroyed. Many others' homes were destroyed, and they suffered from loss and grief. Those who didn't lose their homes felt survivor's guilt. Everyone suffered with one form or another of trauma or PTSD. It took time to recover.

A full year later, some people were rebuilding their homes, others left and sold their empty lots. Most of my friends chose to move away. In fact, I moved, too. I was worried about fires, so I moved away from the forests. This story shows how some of Jack's friends moved away, too. Sadly, things are never quite the same after a disaster, but I wanted to tell others that recovery is possible, feelings of fear eventually leave and joy will return.

One of the surprising things about a wildfire, or any natural disaster, is that many people want to label the cause as one thing. When one is a survivor of a disaster, it is stressful and confusing to listen to outsiders' analysis. *Escape from the Wildfire* attempts to show that a disaster has many contributing factors as well as many unknowns. Wildfires often happen in a natural cycle. Indigenous peoples have long managed these cycles by initiating "burns," which prevent fires from harming communities. The good news is that people are again listening to that wisdom. People are adaptable, and scientists believe that people can adjust to changing climate by building homes in new ways to withstand weather in their area. In addition, creating cleaner energy for homes and vehicles and conserving wild places will protect biodiversity, which safeguards the Earth's resiliency.

Surviving a disaster can produce feelings of euphoria and thankfulness to be alive, and a permanent change in how one views life. The story ends with Jack and his friends enjoying the forest as it begins to grow back, and he states, "We are survivors." Thinking of one's self not as a victim but as a survivor helps to foster a sense of well-being.

A few years after purchasing an acreage with hardly any trees as a reaction to surviving a wildfire, my family and I have planted more than forty trees. And we plan to plant many more trees in the years to come. Trees love to consume carbon, so they help to offset people's carbon consumption.

What is true and what is fiction in the story? All the people in the story are fictitious, except for the mayor of Lytton. The dates, temperatures and place names of Lytton, Lillooet, Merritt, Boston Bar, the school, Chinese Museum and Blue Jays team are real. Details were taken from news reports, videos shared on the internet, Google Maps and related websites. Forestry and tree planting details came from a forestry expert based in British Columbia (who wishes to remain anonymous). Climate and weather science were discussed with university professor Dr. Stephen Jeans. Details specific to the Lytton and Merritt areas were clarified with Jeff Bloom, a retired teacher and author who lives in Merritt. Where there was a lack of information, the author used her experiences and imagination.

The escape scene is exaggerated for dramatic effect, and I took a guess as to trails around the area based on how my own kids rode on any available trails as well as how they built jumps. The swimming hole adjacent to Lytton is imagined and based on river-swimming experiences I shared with my family at the Clearwater River in Alberta. The date of the bus tour for Lytton residents was changed to an earlier day to work better with the characters in the story. The intention was to tell a story with compassion while conveying the real impacts on people.

ACKNOWLEDGEMENTS

Appreciation goes to James Lorimer, publisher, and Allister Thompson, children's editor, for believing in this story, along with the fantastic team at Lorimer Kids & Teens, including copy editor Megan Kearns and assistant editor Sara Rodgers, for their guidance through the story refining process.

Gratitude goes to the forestry expert located in the interior of British Columbia for teaching me about forestry, tree planting and wildfire management. Much appreciation goes to Stephen Jeans, PhD., my university geography professor, for feeding my love of nature by making the study of Earth enjoyable, and for taking time with a former student to discuss the complexities of climate and biodiversity. A shout out to Jeff Bloom, a children's author who lives in Merritt, B.C., for providing feedback specific to the Lytton and Merritt areas.

Last but never least, I am also grateful to my family. My sons, Aaron and Garrett, provided suggestions on how Jack might see and experience life. My husband, Jeff, has been endlessly patient and loving while I lived with the almost constant appendage of a laptop. And my daughter, Chloe, reminds me to pursue my dreams.

On a final note of support and encouragement to the residents of Lytton and area, I believe Lytton will be beautiful again. Stay strong. You can do this.

Ten per cent of the author's income from this book will be donated to the village of Lytton to aid with recovery. Donate at Lytton.ca.

STUDY QUESTIONS

1. Consider the main character, Jack. At the start of the story, what does he care about? How do his interests change by the end of the book? What causes him to change?

2. Who are the secondary characters in the story? Are they stereotypical characters, or are they unique and dynamic? Explain your answers.

3. Contrast Jack with his two best friends. How do their lives and character development differ? What important changes happen to each of them? Do the changes bring them closer together, or take them farther apart?

4. As Jack's interest in Tess grows, how do her interests influence his?

5. Explore the setting of the story. Look at Google Maps satellite images of the location and surrounding areas. How did the location of Lytton inform the story? Is the setting a character, too?

6. How does the setting influence the interests of the characters? Could the events of the story happen anywhere, or are they specific to the location?

7. Notice the colours of t-shirts in the story. How do they reflect the moods of the story?

8. Consider the point of view the author used to tell the story. Did she use first person, second person or third person? Does the POV shift in different parts of the story?

9. What is present tense, past tense and future tense? Does the tense shift in different parts? If so, give examples and explain why the author may have chosen to use different tenses.

10. What does Jack believe about trees in the story? What does he think about his father's work in forestry, and his friend Tess's biodiversity club?

11. Did you find contradictions in the story? If so, how? Does Jack contradict himself? Analyze any contradictions you find and decide if two things can both be true at the same time.

12. What is climate and what is weather? Define these two terms and note any differences.

13. Can people predict the weather? Can people predict the climate? If so, what methods are used?

14. Consider the age of the Earth. How long have people kept records of the weather and the overall climate of the Earth? What are some good sources to read about weather and climate?

15. How is the imagery of mountain lions used in the story?

16. Do all the characters in the story relate the same way to the wildfire and to its aftermath? If not, what may prompt different responses?

17. Find information regarding the First Nations peoples of the interior of British Columbia. What are their band names? How long have they inhabited the land? How did they survive on the land before settlers moved to the land?

18. Choose one Indigenous tribe and describe their ceremonies, their spiritual beliefs and their artistic practices. What are some artifacts that could be found in Kumsheen, or Lytton?

19. Research the earliest records available about Chinese Canadian railway workers. Can you find the photo of the *Last Spike* Jack wrote about? What were their living conditions like?

20. Compare living in the Thompson-Nicola Valley today with when rail companies built train tracks. How has the population changed? How have the lifestyles of the people changed? What kinds of developments made life easier? What kinds of developments have made life worse for people?

21. If you had to design a weather-proof house that uses clean energy, what would it look like, and what materials would you use?

22. Have you experienced a natural disaster? If so, what did you learn about yourself during the experience? What did you learn about the Earth, and about its processes?

23. Read about Lytton and their recovery process at Lytton.ca.

If you or someone you know has experienced trauma through wildfire or another natural disaster, speak with your parent, a teacher or school counsellor. There is help available.

RECOMMENDED RESOURCES FOR FURTHER STUDY

Climate

- *How Ice Ages Happen, The Milankovitch Cycles* (https://www.youtube.com/watch?v=iA788usYNWA). Explains climate and weather influences on a broader scale.
- *Can We Cool The Planet?* NOVA documentary (https://www.youtube.com/watch?v=PeYJTluQ5tM). Suggests technological solutions.
- *Protect Your Home from Wildfire* (https://www2.gov.bc.ca/assets/gov/public-safety-and-emergency-services/wildfire-status/prevention/prevention-home-community/bcws_homeowner_firesmart_manual.pdf).

Biodiversity

- Learn about how trees help the environment (https://treecanada.ca/resources/).
- Biological diversity in Canada, with short film and government goals (https://www.canada.ca/en/environment-climate-change/services/biodiversity.html).
- *Wildfires 101* (https://www.youtube.com/watch?v=5hghT1W33cY). *National Geographic* movie.
- *The Big Little Farm*, movie (https://www.biggestlittlefarmmovie.com/).

Earth-Friendly Products

In the story, Jack mentions that his sister Quinn makes her own shampoo and soap. Here are videos on making your own earth-friendly products:

- Make your own shampoo (https://www.healthline. com/health/homemade-shampoo).
- Make your own laundry soap (https://www.youtube. com/watch?v=B39F514tS58).

Plant a tree!

Did you know that trees love to absorb carbon? Dorothy wrote the character Tess to mirror her own love of trees. She and her family have planted close to fifty trees to date. Plant a tree in your yard or with your class. (OMIT the rest.)

Join or Start a Biodiversity Club

Why not start a club at your school? Alternatively, find a related club in your area. There are nature clubs, biodiversity clubs, naturalists, and conservation groups in many areas. Here are a few examples:

- UBC Nature Club: https://beatymuseum.ubc.ca/visit/ nature-club/
- Conservation Bytes: https://conservationbytes. com/2012/10/11/the-biodiversity-club/
- Hamilton's Naturalists' Club: https://hamiltonnature. org/activities/biodiversity/
- Bruce Trail Conservancy: https://torontobrucetrail-club.org/conservation/biodiversity-team

Invite the Author

Invite Dorothy to speak about topics in the story at your school or club. Find details at dorothybentley.ca.